HABILIS

HABILIS

— A NOVEL —

ALYSSA QUINN

DZANC
BOOKS

DZANC BOOKS

2580 Craig Rd.
Ann Arbor, MI 48103
www.dzancbooks.org

Library of Congress Cataloging-in-Publication Data Available upon Request

First US edition: September 2022
Interior design by Michelle Dotter

Printed in the United States of America

10   9   8   7   6   5   4   3   2   1

For Mum

"It may be important for us to know where we came from, but if we can't answer that question scientifically, we can't answer it. If you want to tell stories, well then, tell stories."

—*Noam Chomsky*

"All desire is a desire to be."

—*Rene Girard*

The museum is a discotheque. From every nine o'clock p.m. to two o'clock a.m., display cases slosh violet with light and the wall text bulges and strobes. *Martini, please,* says a woman, and a martini appears. *With a twist,* she says, and now there is a curl of lemon ribbon. She fingers the wide aperture of her glass, little trill of acrylic nail, and thinks of how wonderfully language sometimes works. *Cigarette?* asks a friend. *Yes, please.* The flick of a zippo. Sadsweet smoke of tobacco and clove. Paper crackling to ash.

Exhibit: Olduvai Hominid 7

Here we have the type specimen of the species *Homo habilis*, earliest member of the genus *Homo*. Also known as OH 7, this specimen consists of a fragmented lower mandible with thirteen teeth, isolated maxillary molar, two parietal bones, and twenty-one finger, hand, and wrist bones. He is a boy. Twelve. Maybe thirteen. Look closely and you'll see the Serengeti sunrise, grasses bloodied with light, the naked child running across plain. He chases an egret, wings sheer against a pink shock of sky. He lifts his face, follows the bird until it dissolves into light. The sun is mounting. He closes his eyes against its brightness but leaves his face still lifted, lets his eyelids warm. Then some clockwork inside of him says, *Time to go home.* So home he goes, back across the plain, down the ravine near the river. He has come this way many times, the land knows his footfalls, but today, somehow, is different. Perhaps he loses his footing down the steep side of the ravine. Perhaps he is startled by a wildcat, its teeth jutting like icicles over lip. Or perhaps who knows, but somehow, today, the boy dies. He dies and his family comes looking, and over his body his mother keens, moans, bellows a wordless loss into the air. A cloud of swallows startles from a nearby tree, flits away like a puff of smoke. The family does not bury their child, such rites do not exist, but they move his body off, away from where they live and eat and flake stones into tools. And the body lies there in the soil, let's say next to a patch of African violets, why not, and his flesh rots off, nails and teeth loosen and drop, organs turn to liquid, he stinks. Eventually all the soft tissue is gone, leaving just skeleton behind, the bones disarticulated, untouching, the body no longer bound by ligament and sinew, and finally the bones too begin to go, the acidic soil making a slow meal of them, until at some point, let's say fortuitously, a volcano twenty miles from the ravine erupts, soaks the earth in soft hot ash, and this happens again and again over the millennia, and though most of the boy's skeleton dissolves to dust, certain parts are preserved: a mandible with thirteen teeth, an isolated molar, two parietal bones, twenty-one finger, hand, and wrist bones. And these bones stay packed in their volcanic ash for ages, until, let's say miraculously, a team of researchers cuts into the earth and, so slowly, with such care, reveals the boy's old bones. They pull him from the earth at last, once again under the Serengeti sun, and they call him OH 7, Olduvai Hominid 7, and estimate he would have had a brain size of 663 cubic centimeters, had he lived to maturity, and they name him the type specimen of a brand-new species, habilis, *Homo habilis,* "handy man." They touch his mandible with gloved fingers and imagine his life, his death, imagine their DNA spiraling back toward him, across this gulf of time.

The woman's name is Lucy. She has drained her martini, smoked the last of her clove, and now watches the bodies dancing around her, their blue slick of sweat, silver fistfuls of disco light spangling skin. At the center of the floor the bodies merge and fuse, a silhouetted mass with a million limbs. Her friend, Dina, stirs a whiskey ginger and says, *It's radical I know, but we were facing bankruptcy. Plus, the bones were getting lonely.* Lucy can feel the music beating in her pelvis. Her bones, humming like a bass drum. *It was not an easy sell, let me tell you,* says Dina. *Our board of directors are practically fossils themselves.* Dina is dressed in her red curator's blazer and checkered black-and-white shorts, the long black mop of her hair pulled back into a thick ponytail. Blue light smears her cheek like oil paint, darkening in the recesses of her jawline, the curve of her nose. *Come on,* she says. Tosses back the last of her drink and grabs Lucy's hand. *Let's dance.*

Exhibit: Antelope metapodial bone

One and a half million years old. Behind the glass, a soft and woody brown, eroded edges revealing a lattice of loam. Think back to when this bone was carcass. Wide gash in tawny fir, blood thick and dripping. The smell. Nearby, a dozen protohumans (male) lift their heads and catch the coppery whiff of meat. They follow it to its source and find the animal, newly dead and unclaimed, splayed and red and waiting. All that gorgeous meat, that creamy marrow. The protohumans' pupils swell and saliva floods their mouths, but there are too many of them for this small corpse. And each one starts toward the prize, hands up and out—then stops. Looks around the circle of large dark eyes and sees desire mirrored everywhere. They pause, hands hanging, and think of what is about to happen, what has already happened so many times—the bashed skulls and shredded skin—and somewhere deep inside them, some quirk of DNA, some evolutionary adjustment whispers, *Stop.* And then the hands that lifted with the intention of grabbing, claiming, seizing, are instead only pointing—pointing to the carcass at their center. To point. To point is not to grasp. It is to say: *This. This. This.* To substitute gesture for meat, for marrow, for blood. To posit a mind not your own, a gaze not your own. It is to become, suddenly, human.

On the dance floor. The throb of light and sound. Time swells like a balloon, then pops, shrinks to a point. Bodies bodies bodies. Or just one body. One large body, lacking symmetry, lacking center, ecstatic, catatonic, pulsing. Her skin becomes his skin becomes your skin becomes mine. There is sweat on her lip and it tastes like a stranger. There are hands around her and they float without origin. Reach for them. Thread sweaty fingers together like tapestry. That space between fingers—it should have a name. For every finger, a corresponding negative space. We are like puzzle pieces, she thinks, she wants to believe. Around her, metacarpals and phalanges stretch and splay—long, loping, knobbly with knuckle. Prehensile: able to grasp or hold. But also: able to let go. Able to lose. *Please hold your child's hand.* Her first girlfriend refused to hold her hand in public. They walked with fingers hanging in space, occasionally a brushed thumb. *Please hold your child's hand while entering or exiting the train.* Hands are what is held, are what do the holding. A closed loop. *Please. Please hold your child. Please hold your child's hand.*

Lucy looks for Dina in the throng. Finds her. Locks eyes on the nape of her neck.

Exhibit: Lower Paleolithic Oldowan tool set

The oldest stone tools, used by *Homo habilis* and *Homo ergaster*. First discovered by anthropologists Louis and Mary Leakey at Olduvai Gorge in Tanzania. Here you will see three different kinds of tool, though classification is fraught. Mary Leakey first sorted the tools into the following types: choppers, scrapers, and pounders. Subsequent taxonomists, however, objected to assuming *use* from *manufacture*. As such, new classifications include: flaked pieces, detached pieces, pounded pieces, unmodified pieces. The new classifications warn: you do not know these people. The flaked pieces whisper: imagination is a lie. Pounded pieces insist: nothing is universal.

Paleoanthropologists have repeatedly reconstructed the Oldowan tool-making process for academic purposes. Here's how: strike a spherical hammerstone against the edge of a suitable core rock (preferably of quartz, basalt, obsidian, flint, or chert). You will find these rocks among river cobbles, where the water has washed them round and smooth and the size of your fist. You will collect them, perhaps, in the early dawn, before the sun is hot, while the wildebeest graze and the acacia trees drip with dew. You will turn them over and over in your newly dexterous fingers, feel the heft and grain, begin to imagine what shapes this stone could take. Then you will strike the core rock, again and again, producing a conchoidal fracture. The chip removed is called the flake. It will leave ripples in its wake, concentric curves that form a hollow—little obsidian pocket—the shape of absence. This process is called *lithic reduction* and illustrates the fact that what is lost always forms the boundary of what is.

Please hold your child's hand while entering or exiting the train. The voice is robotic, female. The interior of the train stings bright as bleach. A child cries. Eighteen months old and the only passenger in this car. She wears pink boots, a winter coat far too large. She is standing on the gangway connector and with every turn in the tracks the floor rotates at her feet. She cannot keep her balance, skins her hands when she falls. The train rockets through the dark. A trajectory she will never remember.

In the body heat and beat of strobe, Lucy feels lightheaded. The bones don't help—hollow sockets eyeless and gaping, cracked teeth jutting in gappy grins. She reaches for Dina's arm. Skin hot slick. *I'm going to the place with the sinks*, she says. *What?* Dina shouts back. Lucy blinks. Puts a hand to her head. *The bathroom*, she says. *I'm going. To the bathroom.*

Exhibit: Forkhead Box Protein P2

Better known as FOXP2. Check out the shape of this thing—like the contents of a party cracker right after it's pulled. So many intricate parts: zinc finger and leucine zipper, alpha helix and beta strands. Can you believe that these amino ribbons are what make language work? That this protein, hanging out on the q arm of chromosome seven, allows you to say, *Could you pass the butter, please?* And lo, the butter appears.

1987, West London. Seven cousins are all enrolled in the special education program at Brentford Primary School. The children's speech is all wrong. Consonants dropped all over the place—*book* becomes *ook*, *blue* becomes *bu*. They stutter, too, words turning choppy and disrupted as their tongues hang forever on a single syllable, unable to pivot to the next. The mouth and tongue are normally so intelligent. Example: say the word *happy*. Before you have said anything, you will already be breathing out, you will have moved your tongue into position and opened your mouth in anticipation of the *a*. Then, even as you are hissing for *h*, the *h* will have something of the shape of an *a*, so that when you stop hissing, there it is, that round and ready vowel. And as soon as your mouth is fully open for *a*, you will already be closing it again, your lips meeting for *p*, and while your lips are together for *p*, your tongue is retreating to get ready for *y*, so that as you separate your lips in a tiny puff of air, the *y* is there, waiting to seal the word up. The whole thing takes less than half a second, even though pronouncing the vowels and consonants individually would take much longer. Time travel exists in these overlapping sounds, in this space between your lips.

But not for the seven cousins at Brentford Primary, and not for half their family, going back three generations or more. Their teacher, learning of this family history, calls up a geneticist at the Institute of Children's Health, and the next thing the kids know they're in a lab with blood pressure cuffs around their biceps and needles piercing the crooks of their arms. Fourteen years later, it's confirmed: a language gene, one of several perhaps, but nonetheless we've found proof of this at least—that language is carried in our blood.

The bathrooms are soaked in blue. Indigo LED coming down in cones. Everything looks underwater and Lucy feels she may float upward like a bubble. Washing her hands, she looks in the mirror and jumps. Behind her, a female *Homo habilis* stares. Unblinking. Despite the soft pelt of her skin and long swing of her arms, Lucy knows her as kin. In the thick light they stare at each other. Fogged reflections, completely still.

EXHIBIT: MITOCHONDRIAL DNA, 10,000,000X MAGNIFICATION

Squint and you'll see it. Faint smudge behind glass. Mitochondrial DNA is inherited only through the mother, leading to the concept of Mitochondrial Eve, the most recent woman from whom all humans descend, linked to us through our mothers and our mothers' mothers, a lineage of wombs, going back and back and back and back and back.

Back perhaps to this *Homo habilis* in the blue bathroom of the museum that is a discotheque. She and Lucy staring at each other in the mirror. Tap water running. Hands suspended over the sink. She wants to speak but how can she. And outside, Dina waits, throbbing with music and light, bourbon on her breath. Lucy shuts off the faucet with a squeak. Exits the bathroom and doesn't look back.

EXHIBIT: CHILD LANGUAGE ACQUISITION

How to explain this mundane magic? All over the world, babes opening their mouths to form first words. Often, it is to name a desire. *Mama. Juice.* Or frequently: *No.* The name for desire that conflicts with another.

The poverty of the stimulus theory goes like this: every day, all over the world, sentences are spoken that have never been spoken before. From a limited number of examples, an unlimited number of speech acts. We must be built for this, the linguists reason. Our brains must be hardwired for words.

So track it. Mother, father, and baby arrive home for the first time. In the ceiling of every room, a fish eye camera and a microphone. Recording twenty-four hours a day, every day. *Hey, welcome home, little guy.* Every moment, every word.

1. *Audio time lapse of the word "water"*: listen as *gaaaa*, becomes *gagaa, gaga, gagu, gadu, wadu, wada, wader, wa-tur*, and finally, finally, *water*. Listen to the word blossom, six months compressed into forty seconds. Listen to the boy become human.

2. *Caregiver feedback loops*: and once a new word is learned, we go back into the record, locate every instance of the word the boy has ever heard. Record the length and complexity of the sentence in which the word is found. And here, the remarkable pattern: sentence complexity dips to its lowest point at the precise moment the baby first learns the new word. Every time. As if the mother and father can

sense the word about to roll off their son's small tongue; as if they are restructuring their sentences to meet him at the word's birth; only after which do they slowly increase their sentences' complexity again, bringing him carefully with them. Baby learning from environment, environment from baby. A level of attention you can hardly believe is real.

3. *Wordscapes of baby's first ten words*: motion tracking follows mother, father, and baby as they move throughout their home. In the footage, they trail red, yellow, and blue lines of color, respectively. When a new word is learned, we return to the record, find every instance of that word and identify *where* it was uttered. The end result: something akin to a topographic map—peaks and valleys indicating word frequency, sketching the relation between language and its habitat. *Water* peaks in the kitchen. *Bye* near the door. *Mama* is scattered all throughout the halls. A world drawn in words.

So yes. Language lives in blood and brain. But it is not just a thing locked up inside us. Language exists at our surface; the place where inside becomes out.

Dina is back at the bar, swirling skinny black straws in a second whiskey ginger. Lucy wades through the thick blue crowd, past the display cases piling up with highballs, ice cubes glowing pink, orange, green. Dina is chatting with a man in a plain grey suit, a rainbow sequin bowtie added like an afterthought. *The disco thing was actually the selling point. Pitched it as a historical artifact in and of itself. Disco to them feels retro, vintage. What they don't realize is disco was majorly subversive back then, once. You know, deviant—at the beginning.* Lucy orders another martini with a twist. It arrives with an olive. Heavy on the brine. *You've seen the diorama? At the entrance? I helped with it.* Light peels off in misty petals from Lucy's glass. The olive stares, a bleached green eye, red pimento pupil. Dina starts suddenly and says, *God, sorry, I'm so rude. This is Lucy. Lucy, Nathan. He's an evolutionary psychologist*—she articulates every syllable disconnected from the rest—*and a patron.* They nod, raise their glasses toward each other. Lucy drains her drink, grimaces—she's never liked olives. *Disgust,* says Nathan. *Excuse me? Your expression,* he says. *That's disgust.* She wonders if she is meant to congratulate him. *I don't like the green things,* she says. *You mean olives? Yes. Olives. Disgust is fascinating,* says Nathan. *From an evolutionary perspective.* Lucy frowns, but he keeps going. *Did you know disgust and aggression are inversely correlated? Because disgust prompts withdrawal, rather than confrontation.* Lucy's mouth is still briny and slick, nostrils flared, lips puckered. *Fun fact,* says Nathan. *Women are more sensitive to disgust than men.* Women are women are women are.

Exhibit: Pelvic bone, *Australopithecus afarensis*

A butterfly of bone. Nothing will ever seem more alien to you than the shape of your own pelvis. Calcium cradle you cannot believe you contain. But you do.

The *Australopithecus* pelvis is wider than ours but narrower than a chimp's. The shrinking pelvis, a product of bipedalism. Walking upright has its advantages; on the wide flat of the savannah, you can spot predators from miles away. Your hands free up, too, allowing you to carry tools and food, allowing in turn for the protein-rich diet required for a growing brain. But these advantages demanded the body change its shape, and no one felt this change more than the women. The birth canal narrowed, and to compensate, babies were born earlier, smaller, less developed. Fontanelles soft as bruised fruit. These children needed to be carried and cared for, years longer than their primate counterparts. All those upright mothers, tethered to the earth by offspring and pain.

Foundling. That's the word for what she is. Worse than *orphan,* which has a certainty to it. Foundling gapes. Even the shape of the mouth when it's uttered—opening like a hole around all those vowels. She dreams of trains at night, even though she cannot possibly remember. The rickety rhythm of railway ties. Like bones being strummed. *I gave her a lollipop from my pocket.* An orphan, or even a child given up for adoption, can trace an origin. Birth parents exist, hidden at the end of a trail of clues, waiting only for excavation. *It was butterscotch. From a trip to the bank.* Even others like her can usually point to a location: *I was left at the bus station in Greenwich. I was discovered on the doorstep of the fire station.* They could return to that place of origin, sit on a park bench and scan the crowd for familiar genes. But a train is only shifting space. Fluid. All she knows is she was deposited on the Metro-North somewhere between Poughkeepsie and Yonkers, sometime between the hours of 7:30 and 9 p.m. on November 6, 1991. She knows it was raining. She knows an MTA police officer found her and *handed her the unwrapped sucker. But she just kept crying. I tried to pick her up but she cried harder and harder. I radioed it in right away, of course, and backup met us Ludlow. A female officer, thank god. Managed to get her off the train. Then took her away to the hospital, social services, the rest. And I stood there on the platform with that unwrapped butterscotch sucker.* She knows the moon was new.

Which makes sense, he continues. *Given women's need to be more se-lective with a mate.* Here, Dina snorts. *What?* Nathan asks. His voice defensive. Women are women are. *It's true,* he says. *It's empirical.* Dina tips the ice cubes from her glass into her mouth, shifts them into one cheek and says, *Fuck empiricism.* She grabs Lucy's hand again and says, *Come see that diorama.* But as Lucy turns around, there she is again. Against a far wall, dark eyes piercing. Lucy re-coils and Dina looks at her, inquiring. Those dark eyes. She cannot read them. Are they angry? Accusatory? Sorry? Sad? Welcoming her home or casting her out? *Mary, Mary, m a r y, M A R Y.* A glut of chipped obsidian. A teakettle shriek. *You okay?* Lucy blinks. Rubs her eyes. The woman is gone. *Yeah.* The DJ has just switched the song and the bass is something deep and primal. *I'm okay.*

Exhibit: Diorama, Disco Demolition Night, July 12, 1979

Admire the workmanship here—not easy, since the wall is a single curved plane. This eliminates corners and seams, allows the wall to disappear, to dissolve, but it poses a challenge for the artist, who must work extra hard to minimize all distortion. Their job is to create depth where none exists, texture when so much is surface, to conjure the thick heat of that July night. That sky still violently blue even at six p.m., those green stripes of the baseball field lashing like a whip. The teal plastic seats of Comiskey Park are filling up quick—40,000 spectators and still they're swarming through the gates like ants. In their respective dugouts, the Chicago White Sox and Detroit Tigers eye each other. Stretch their calves. Chomp wads of pink gum. It's been a bad season for the White Sox, with only 15,000 in attendance at last night's game. But the team's promotions director has been racking his brains. One night, sitting at the kitchen table with his third or fourth beer, radio turned to the rock station, he hears the host blow up a disco record on air. The promotions director guffaws, cheers, smacks a hand onto the Formica. He sure *hates* disco. And then he has an idea, and he's up, out of his chair, calling his manager, saying, *Get a load of this.* The idea: an anti-disco rally to promote their doubleheader with the Tigers. Bring a disco record and you'll be admitted for just 98 cents. Then, in between the two games, we'll blow 'em up on field. They get the rock station to sponsor the event, and on the radio, the host sings parodies on air: *Do you think I'm disco / 'cause I spend so much time / blow drying out my hair / Do you think I'm disco / 'cause I know the dance steps I learned 'em all at Fred Astaire.* And now there are 50,000 and they're closing the gates but people are still squeezing in through the cracks, leaping over turnstiles, climbing fences, being lifted through windows by friends already inside. At the far end of the park, the scoreboard bears ads for Union 76, Kool super light cigarettes, and a brand of canned cocktails touted as "Iced n' Easy." The air stinks so thickly of beer it nearly bubbles, so heavy with pot smoke it wobbles like mirage. Massive banners ripple in the crowd: DISCO SUCKS. LONG LIVE ROCK N ROLL. They are young and white and male. They are all sweat and heat and reefers and rage.

An usher, a fourteen-year-old Black boy, eyes the pile of records by the door. Thousands. Black gloss like onyx. They're not all disco records. In fact, they're mostly not disco records. They're mostly Black records. He sees a few names he recognizes from the radio and, when no one's looking, swipes a couple and stows them in his locker. In the crowd, some people are still holding their records—there were simply too many to collect. It's the ninth inning, the White Sox are losing, people are getting impatient, and now a few of them start to fling the records like frisbees. They slice past players' heads and crater into the ground, sticking up at canted angles. Finally the game ends. The radio host rides onto the field in a jeep. He wears army fatigues, a camo combat helmet, aviator glasses. In the heavy heat, his longish hair glues to his forehead, the back of his neck. He leads the crowd in a chant: DIS-CO SUCKS. DIS-CO SUCKS. The crowd writhes and roars. Delirious. *This is now officially the world's largest anti-disco rally!* screams the radio host. *Now listen—we took all the disco records you brought tonight, we got 'em in a giant box, and we're gonna blow 'em up—REAL. GOOD.* Comiskey Park just minutes from Bridgeport, one of the whitest neighborhoods in Chicago, where the young usher's white girlfriend lives. Walking her home last weekend, a car pulled up alongside him, slowed to a crawl. Lowered its window. *Where do you think you're going?* And goddamn did he run—like the track star he was training to be. But they were faster. The slam of the car doors closing—one, two, three. The sidewalk, rough and dusty. The sky overhead heavy as a quilt in summer. *REAL GOOD,* yells the radio host. *REAL. GOOD.*

The box blows—red-orange flare, upward tumble of smoke. Records rocket through the air, black vinyl shrapnel with edges like obsidian. The radio host does a victory slide on his knees. Punches the air. At an interview a few days later, he will say, *It's an intimidating lifestyle, it's an intimidating culture, and it was being forced down our throats.* He'll smash a record on his head till it shatters. The crowds are leaving the bleachers now and swarming the field. Security cannot stop them. Five thousand. Then seven. They dig the bases from the soil. Slide down foul poles. Pitch cherry bombs and beer bottles through the air. The young Black usher and his coworkers are told to get out of here—go to their lockers. They grip their flashlights like weapons and run. The crowd knocks over the batting cage, sets it on fire. They remove their shirts and seven thousand white torsos gleam under the bright stadium bulbs. The usher, running to his locker, is stopped by a shirtless white man who brandishes a record in his face and shouts, *See this?* Then breaks it over his knee. After nearly forty minutes, the Chicago police arrive and issue 39 arrests. But the field is left scarred as a battleground. Unplayable. The White Sox forfeit the second game.

Afterward, the white men say: *Disco is the bane of our existence.*

They say: *All flash and no substance. Giant wardrobes to make themselves into different people. A bunch of phonies.*

They say: *It's like an assault on what we grew up with.*

They say: *A little bit of a battle. An us-and-them mentality.*

Overnight, disco drops from the air. The nightclubs become country western bars. *I saw the writing on the wall,* says one owner. *I bought a mechanical bull.*

The radio host says: *I have no prejudices. People say it was racist and homophobic. But it wasn't.*

One of the men who assaulted the usher is the Bridgeport police chief's son. They offer the boy fifty bucks to drop the charges, and the boy, who is saving up for a synthesizer, accepts.

The radio host says: *I think for the most part everything was wonderful.*

I glued the records in, see? says Dina. *But we hired a retired diorama artist to do most of the real work.* The scene features a baseball diamond, several men standing on the field with a microphone and a giant (although actually tiny) crate of vinyl records. The perspective positions viewers as if they are sitting in the bleachers—at the edge is a row of full-size plastic seats, facing the field, and everything beyond shrinks slowly in proportion to its distance, so that the figures on the field are only five or six inches tall and the records are like dinner plates for dolls. *This guy—he was like eighty. And just kept telling the same story over and over again, about dioramas, how they're a dying art form, can't keep up with all these new pyrotechnic museum exhibits. Kept talking about all these dioramas that have fallen into disrepair, or been dismantled and stripped for parts. A bonobo exhibit in some natural history museum he visited in which all the bonobos lay face down in their fake dirt, nobody had even bothered to right them. Which is genuinely depressing.*

Lucy was asked to create a genealogical diorama in the sixth grade. The life of an ancestor squeezed into a shoebox. After some cajoling, she chose her then-foster mom's maternal grandmother, who was apparently part of the Polish underground during WWII, before she emigrated to America. The family story, which Lucy has since learned to question, is that this grandmother blew up a bunch of German radio stations along the Danube. This, at any rate, was the scene she depicted. The river, crumpled blue tissue paper. The woman, a miniature porcelain doll that was nevertheless much too large for the toothpick-and-string radio towers. Heaps of rice for snow. She and her foster mom spent hours on that damn shoebox. Then, on her way to school, she fell and its contents launched across the street. *The poor guy said he'd retired rather than be part of this dismantling. I don't think he liked it when he learned about the button.* Dina reaches out and presses a big red button mounted near the diorama's description and a plume of smoke and a few flashes of light emanate from the tiny box of records. A man's voice issues from a speaker: *Blow it up—REAL. GOOD.* The smoke clots thick and sulfuric in Lucy's lungs.

What does this have to do with anything? They turn around and Nathan is there again. *I mean, it just feels a little out of place.*

Dina folds her arms. Lucy would like to say that it is not out of place at all, that it fits, it fits exactly. But the words are all confused on her tongue.

EXHIBIT: SIMA DE LOS HUESOS, ATAPUERCA, SPAIN

Translated as the "Pit of Bones." At the bottom of a 43-foot vertical shaft in a cave in the hills of Atapuerca, over 6,000 hominid fossils lie in a heap. This is the resting place of 28 early humans—*Homo heidelbergensis,* probably—and, at 350,000 years old, is the earliest sign we have of ritual burial. Amid the skeletons (imagine them, all mixed up in each other's femurs and teeth) lies a single hand ax, unique among tools of this period, in that it is colored pink like a sunset, hand-daubed with pigment. And from this color, *Homo sapiens* hundreds of thousands of years later construct a story. The hand ax, they say, isn't just a hand ax; it is a symbol, it is a rite, cast into the Pit of Bones on a tide of mythology and belief. In this pink tool they see the origins of culture, religion, philosophy.

Here is one theory of the evolution of language: it is useful, yes, to be able to say, *There is a leopard near the river.* It is useful to be able to say, *I found fruit growing over there.* Useful to be able to label your world, pin words to it like markers on a compass, share its reality with others and thus live a little longer. Useful, too, to gossip, form alliances, trade information about group members, about whom you are able to trust. But as human groups expanded, it became impossible to know everybody intimately. You can only gossip effectively about roughly 150 people, it turns out. And so another kind of sentence evolved. Sentences like, *The leopard spirit is the guardian of our tribe.* Like, *The creator gods demand a sacrifice.* Like, *The Dow Jones is down 84 points this morning.* Sentences about things that do not exist at all. Sentences like a pink hand ax laid in a grave.

It's the sentences about things that do not exist at all that allowed human groups to function. Myths and legends, governments and religions, currencies and corporations. All collective fictions human beings lumped into their language, alongside leopards and rivers and fruit growing ripe on the limb.

So come up close; lean over the edge; peer down into the dark. Maybe you'll catch the calcium glint, the shape of empty eyes that look almost like your own. Or maybe you'll just pretend.

Lucy must be getting increasingly drunk because they are at the bar again and there is another drink in her hand and she doesn't remember getting there. Nathan the evolutionary psychologist: *I'm not saying I like it. I'm just saying it's* biological. In Lucy's drink there is not an olive but an incisor. Fossilized and worn, its single tapered root a crusty, bark-like brown. Dina puts a hand on her arm and says, *You've met OH 7?* Lucy turns around and there is the mandible with thirteen teeth, isolated molar, parietal, finger, hand, and wrist bones, cobbled strangely together and floating in the air.

Exhibit: Phylogenetic tree with expletives
and the head of Carl Linnaeus

A branching of Latin. Shape of our becoming, with all its roots and rhizomes. And then this: anthropologists shouting at each other in laboratories, on conference panels, perhaps even on site, as they lift the contested fossils from the earth, even then screaming and swearing in defense of an imaginary tree. Look closely, that branch there, *Homo habilis* crossed out and *Australopithecus habilis* scrawled above it. This crossed out in turn, *Homo* added back in, then crossed out again, this time in favor of *Australopithecus afarensis*. *You sir have a bad habit of coining names for fossils that do not deserve them.* The blood rises in the anthropologist's face. *Consider, sir, the ape-like morphology, long limbs, and diminutive stature.* His flush deepens. His nomenclature threatened, his taxa tossed like trash. *I for one hope that "Homo habilis" will disappear as rapidly as he came.*

This fierce marginalia, the tree with its slashes and scars, its battered fruit—all inquire, *What makes a species?* The answer is neither evolution nor god. The answer is: middle-aged men in crumpled white shirts and loosened ties. The answer is: these endless brackets, endless divisions, another species, another: *habilis, rudolfensis, gautengensis, erectus, ergaster, antecessor, heidelbergensis, cepranensis, rhodensis, naledi, neanderthalensis, floresiensis, tsaichangensis, sapiens.* From a few pocked skull shards, a whole new class of creature. *What my colleague does not seem to understand is that when one species evolves into another, there will be a transitionary period in which it resembles neither ancestor nor descendent.* The phylogenetic tree is a fiction. Its fingers reaching for an origin they themselves have built. *Not to mention intra-species variation, which allows A. afarensis to accommodate these new bones comfortably.* So why such pleasure in its shape?

And here, next to the tree, its endpoint, its terminal branch, we have the head of Swedish botanist Carl Linnaeus, finely preserved and taxedermied. Observe the clean white coils of his wig. Eyes closed as if in sleep. Our patron saint, father of modern taxonomy, inventor of *binomial nomenclature*, a phrase you want to say over and over, it fills your mouth sweet and round as an apple. *B i n o m i a l   n o m e n c l a t u r e.* The story goes that, as a boy, little Carl would invariably cheer up if presented with a flower. Perhaps the heavy glossy head of a tulip—red and splashed with black inside. Or perhaps *Linnaea borealis,* his favorite, named for him, in fact, and today the official national flower of Sweden. *Linnaea is a plant of Lapland, lowly, insignificant, disregarded, flowering but for a brief space—after Linnaeus who resembles it,* he writes self-deprecatingly in his *Critica Botanica.* Linnaeus classified over 7,000 species in his lifetime, doling out names like Adam. He spent six months trekking through Lapland, sifting species into order—scrubby lichens, mountain flowers bunched low against the ground, flounder and pike in the brackish waters of the Baltic—and for all his classificatory efforts the Swedish king granted him nobility. His name changed to Carl von Linné and his family received their own coat of arms featuring the delicate pink pendulums of the *Linnaea borealis* and a single large egg at its center. And this is not Linnaeus's only distinction. He is also the type specimen of his species—type specimen of *Homo sapiens.* Every species must have its type, a single specimen to stand for all the rest. He named the species and to the name attached himself. In addition, he identified four subspecies: *europaeus* (governed by laws), *americanus* (governed by customs), *asiaticus* (governed by opinions), and *afer* (governed by impulse).

He himself was included in none of these subspecies, not even *europaeus*, which was described as having "long blond hair, blue eyes," whereas Linnaeus had brown hair, brown eyes. He is emblematic of the species; he is outside the species. Look at him, this fine head. Do you not see yourself? You are Carl Linnaeus. Carl Linnaeus is you.

The bones of OH 7 clink lightly together in the air and Lucy stares. Dina nudges her in the ribs. *Don't be rude,* she whispers. *He's been through a lot, this kid.* Lucy feels suddenly bad. She fishes in her drink and pulls out the fossilized incisor. Holds it out to OH 7. *I think this belongs to you.* OH 7 clinks, clinks, clinks. *He can't speak,* Dina says, still whispering. She taps her throat and practically mouths the words, *No hyoid.* Nathan says, *Our biological realities may not be what we'd like them to be, but they are what they are nonetheless.* The women stare at him. He raises his glass. *Cheers,* he says, and tosses it back.

EXHIBIT: HUMAN HYOID BONE, 300,000 YEARS OLD

Calcium horseshoe, little bone floating in the neck, nestled against larynx, pharynx, epiglottis, but unconnected to the rest of the skeleton. The particular position of the human hyoid allows for a wide range of sounds—a couple thousand phonemes. Nasal, sibilant, fricative, glottal. Diphthongs, plosives, trills, stops. So we comb the earth for these small bones, hoping for the hyoid as some kind of evidence, but the truth is simply this: language is a behavior that doesn't fossilize.

I'm just saying: in a study of 153 sexual encounters, male orangutans utilized aggression 133 times, says Nathan. He has a notebook on his knee, pen poised. Observing the dancing crowd. *That's 87%.* On the floor, Lucy sees men tangled up with men, women with women, groups of three or four or five tangled up together. *Sexual coercion does crazy things to natural selection. Male and female members of the species coevolve, in different directions.* Dina and Lucy share a look like: this guy. *For example, duck penises. These corkscrew-looking things, sixteen inches, spiked surfaces. Just imagine.* And now a look like: umm? *But the vagina has coevolved to thwart it: twists and turns, dead ends, clockwise spirals for the counterclockwise cocks. I mean, don't you just love that?* And for a moment she does—begins to grin—vagina as labyrinth—delightful. *Effective 98% of the time. FDA approved, haha. Still though, it sometimes kills them.* Her grin's gone. Mouth open but empty. *Ducks, beetles, guppies, seals. Lions, dolphins, snakes, cats. Rape is everywhere, and it's shaped our DNA. I'm not saying I like it. I'm just saying it's* biological. He's writing something down in his notebook. Still examining that mass of writhing bodies, the limbs inked with light. What does he read there? What genetic imperative does the strobe beat out like code? She shudders in her skin, skin he acts like he can see straight through, straight through to her cells, to her center, her history, her future. Can he? The music heaves, hot and heavy. She dizzies in the buzzing dark, blinks, can't see, can't speak, can't breathe, can't think. Then a hand on her arm. A voice she knows. *You've met OH 7?* There is a drink in her hand. There are bones in the air.

Sophomore year of college, in bed with her girlfriend Jane, Lucy is awake. Has been awake, listening to Jane breathe, for two hours. Has rolled from her back to her stomach to her back to her side to her stomach. Has curled up next to Jane, slotted against her body like a stacked spoon, then peeled away, too hot and sweat-sticky. Has stared at the ceiling. Has tried not to watch the clock. Has snuck a sidelong glance at the clock after all, panicked to see the numbers sliding swiftly by and sleep no nearer. Tiredness is an itch cinched around her eyeballs, but as tired as she is she still can't *sleep*. Lies on her side, hand under her head, and stares at Jane's ear. The lobe attached. Cartilage coiled in the shape of an embryo. And Lucy is thinking, not for the first time, of the baby they'll never have, the baby that will not have Jane's ears and her nose. She doesn't want kids. Knows this for certain. But still she sometimes does things like stare at her girlfriend's earlobe and think of the DNA curled up inside their cells— DNA that has come down to them across the eons, genes that have morphed and mutated and made it all the way here only to stop. It doesn't bother her, or at least not much. She feels already cut off from the thread of heredity. The lineage spooled in her chromosomes is an abstract concept to her. The line, like something already snapped. But she does think about it, staring at the whorl of skin and shadow that is her lover's ear. And she does not feel sad so much as sealed off. Contained. Like a house locked up. Its blinds shut tight.

    Lucy has never known herself much at all. The inside of her mind always feels inaccessible to her. A blank, dark space. She feels far too deep inside of it to have any sense of what *it* is, to be able to trace its contours, chart its topography. In conversation with others, she finds herself saying things she doesn't think she believes in the hope that one day she might accidentally stumble onto something that rings true. Lying supine on a blanket on a friend's driveway one summer night, a melting tub of orange sherbet, two large spoons. Her friend is reading from a glossy magazine. *What would make you feel most confident on a first date? A) A bold red lip, or B) A spritz of your favorite perfume?* Or like when she looks in the mirror for too long and becomes suddenly hyperaware of the person looking back at her, a person whose privacy she feels she is invading, a person she feels self-conscious around, a person whose face is not her face, no, surely not, and she feels half wild with anxiety upon realizing she is trapped in the skin of this person. *How would your close friends describe you? A) Adventurous and outgoing or B) Sweet and thoughtful?* The tub drips sticky orange melt onto the quilt. The navy sky is speckled with gnats. *A*, says Lucy. *B. A, B, B, A, B, A, A.*

Exhibit: KNM-ER 1470

Such an unfriendly name for a fossil. *Kenya National Museum—East Rudolf.* All we dare say about this shattered skull is where it was found. Cannot agree on whether it's *habilis* or *rudolfensis* or perhaps something else entirely. Several hundred chips of bone, reassembled a dozen different ways. Either the jaw juts out far from the face and the brain has a volume of 526 cubic centimeters, or else the jaw drops straight down and the brain has a volume of 752 cubic centimeters. Shuffle the shards again, a puzzle with half its pieces lost. But there is evidence for this, at least: a bulge in the skull where Broca's Area would be. A bulge of bone that suggests—perhaps—language. In this slight swelling, a story. How can we believe this? But then again—how can we not?

Jar of suckers on the desk. Flat glassy paddles, red orange yellow blue green, curved edges liquidy with light. *Very unusual to see in someone so young.* Picture books on the coffee table behind her. Sendak and Seuss. *I can read with my left eye. I can read with my right. I can read Mississippi with my eyes shut tight.* And on the walls, unobjectionable watercolors. White orchids blurring at the edges. A Thomas Kincaid painting—glowy little cottage, lilac, waterfall, mist. The room holds infancy and old age, stroke victims and toddlers who can't pronounce their Rs, but it knows not what to do with her. *For that reason, I offer the diagnosis somewhat tentatively. Though it is otherwise textbook.* Though not standard, they'd given her an fMRI—slotted her into the massive machine like a bullet into a chamber and asked her a series of questions. *Which shape has three corners? What's the planet closest to the sun? Can you describe your morning routine?* Afterward, they mounted her scans on a box of light and pointed to little red flares mottling her brain like mold. Pointed to Broca's Area, frontal lobe, left hemisphere. *You know what you want to say, you just aren't able. Mississippi, Indianapolis, and Hallelujah, too! I can read them with my eyes shut! That is VERY HARD to do!* Behind the pockets of contrast, her brain a mass of shadow. It looked to her like a Rorschach blot.

EXHIBIT: BYLAWS OF THE LINGUISTIC SOCIETY OF PARIS, ARTICLE II

The Society does not permit any discussion concerning the origin of language.

Thus decreed in 1866, because the question was unanswerable. Unscientific. Embarrassing. A lack of empirical evidence. Language does not fossilize. This is all speculation. This is all lies. Let us not speak of it. Let us leave it in the earth. In the past. In the nothingness whence it came. Leave it there, undisturbed, unknowable, hidden in the dust and dark. Leave it alone.

Leaving the speech pathologist's office with her tentative diagnosis, she stops suddenly in the hospital lobby. People around her converse quietly. The doctors insist her mind is still her mind—her thoughts still lucid, still rational, still her own, even if they are blocked from her lips, blocked from becoming breath and sound, from entering the world. But, nevertheless, for a moment, she forgets who she is. A deepening blankness. The edges of her being smudge, drift, solid as steam. *Most likely a genetic component.* A lion stares at her, huge eyes, from across the lobby. *I need a gift for brain cancer.* The same doctor is being paged over and over on the intercom. The lion is a Mylar balloon. So plastic and shiny.

On a coffee table, she sees a copy of *National Geographic*—knows it first by its yellow border. On the cover is something not quite human, not quite ape. Leathery folds of her face, coarse hair, dark eyes piercing straight through to the grey lobes locked up inside her silent skull. *She's Here: Lucy Tours the U.S.*

And then she's through the automatic doors, across the parking lot, down the street, on the bus, then another bus, then somehow she's purchased a ticket and is sitting on an Amtrak headed from Chicago to New York. Outside, the world is a long green streak. Smudge of speed. The train rocks, rocks, rocks her away.

Lucy and Dina are on the dance floor. The dance floor is a savannah. The disco ball is a white sun rising and the blue light is the morning haze over the caldera. Dina is dancing but Lucy can't. OH 7 still there, at her shoulder, hovering, and she knows he wants something, knows his clinking, which grows steadily louder, is a code, he's calling to her but saying what? *What's wrong?* Dina shouts above the music. Lucy opens her mouth only to find it emptied of words. She knows what she wants to say but the language for it is gone. Her tongue a thick muscle, lying like a corpse in the coffin of her mouth. There is a word, a word, a word for what she means. A word she could seize upon and say out loud that would make Dina understand. She feels herself skirting around it, a flicker of neurons forming a ring at its perimeter, reaching for it, dendrites groping desperate. But they cannot touch it.

So she says, instead, to Dina, *The dead are angry.* But knows immediately this isn't right, because he's not dead, he's here, clinking loud now as a spoon against glass, he is a remnant, a trace, a presence, and so is she, that silent habilis with eyes like stakes. And they aren't angry, not angry, what are they, what are—the clinking is louder and louder, hammer pounding brass nails, she cannot think, the sound is fit to crack her skull and maybe what she meant to say is not *The dead are angry* but *The bones are bitter,* or no, perhaps *The fossils are lost,* closer, closer, maybe she wants to say, *The dance floor is a savannah, the disco ball a sun, our bod-*

ies their bodies. Maybe to speak is to trade one thing for another, always and forever. Maybe her dendrites are like fingers, reaching, reaching, reaching to grasp.

EXHIBIT: INDEX FINGER IN FORMALDEHYDE

The many names: first finger, forefinger, pointer finger, trigger finger, *digitus secundus manus. Index* comes from the Latin *indico,* meaning *to indicate.* The index is the most sensitive of the five fingers. The most dexterous. *Indico* can also be translated as: *announce, betray, proclaim, accuse, appoint, declare, inform, inform against, point out, reveal, show, summon, appraise, disclose, expose, impose, inflict, make known, order, publish, put a price on,* and *value. Indico* can be translated as *to mean.* Babies learn to communicate via pointing around one year old. Pointing can indicate desire, but to wag your pointer finger back and forth is to scold. Desire censured.

In the jar the finger is pale. Bleached of blood. The liquid, once clear, now murky with time. The finger rests on the bottom of the jar. Pointing casually upward. You lift your gaze. Museum spotlight. Blink in the beam.

And think also of an actual index, the back of the book, your finger sliding down alphabetic entries in search of the word you desire. When you find it (if you find it), it will point you elsewhere.

To point entails a gap. Distance between where you are and what you mean. Between what you have and want you want. Between eight and ten months, most babies develop the ability to follow the gaze of another person. Of all the milestones parents mark, this is perhaps the least extolled. But upon this—the ability to *share a gaze*—so much depends. When, for the first time, baby follows mother's eyes. For the first time, attributes a mental reality to this woman whose warmth has kept him cradled. Shared attention. Two individuals focused on the same object at the same time. Upon this depends language acquisition, the establishment of reference, empathy, love. Look at me—now at the object—now me again. Human to object to human. Follow my gaze and I'll follow yours. Follow it and know that the world is at our fingertips, and that which we cannot reach we still can speak of. The starlight in our sky. Enduring for eons. Look—right there—Cassiopeia. And there, Orion. Follow my finger and you'll see.

A half inch of glass. Beyond which, a large dark face. Shaggy hair, sunset orange, ringing the face like an aureole. She's stopped in D.C., her connecting train a few hours away, and is at the National Zoo. The primate house. Five minutes and counting that she and the mother orangutan have been staring at each other through the glass. *Orangutans have long, sparse orange or reddish hair unequally distributed over their bodies. They are the largest arboreal mammals.* God, who writes these things and could they be any less interesting. She and the mother orangutan continue to stare at each other. Seven minutes. The baby orangutan clings to the mother's back. Its elbows are incredibly human. Nine minutes and Lucy begins to cry. Those skinny baby elbows, jutting at sharp angles. Those eyes looking into hers with something she would like to call love. This cold glass, in which she can see her own chilly image, a ghost wedged between them, so backward and brittle.

EXHIBIT: LAST UNIVERSAL COMMON ANCESTOR

The most recent organism from which all life on earth descends. Abbreviated LUCA. LUCA is likely a single cell. Likely contains a solitary coil of DNA floating freely in its cytoplasm. Also likely: RNA, ribosomes, amino acids. The enzymes polymerase and topoisomerase. Likely a membrane made of lipids, semipermeable, to pump ions back and forth. Likely lived in the deepest slots of ocean, where magma kissed the underside of sand.

We extrapolate these features based on what all life shares. What every earthly species has in common. These features you ought to cherish—if you are searching for what it means to be alive, this is it. Ribosomes. Polymerase. Cytoplasm. Here is the answer, the essence, the core from which everything else extends. If LUCA remains mostly mysterious, these things at least are certain. These things bind us together: starfish and the jacaranda tree. E. coli and the prime minister of the United Kingdom. You, reading this text, and me, writing it. LUCA links us to each other. A common reference point. A core, a center, beyond all difference. A single planetary family.

(You may protest that the case is empty. Okay, yes, I apologize. LUCA has a tendency to slip through the fingers. Try as we might to hold it.)

Rain. Red brick. High arched windows with coppery green muntins. This is Poughkeepsie station, nearly a hundred years old, its russet the color of history. And beyond, the Hudson, exact shade and texture of slate. Its impassive face stares at her as if to say, *Why have you come?* The railway tracks, too: *What is it that you want?* A train trundles in and its rattling sounds like all trains everywhere; the long, shrill shriek of its brakes, nothing like a human child. A woman with an umbrella walks by. Her face, obscured.

The dead are angry. And even though this isn't right Dina somehow understands, nods to the beat of the bass. *Trust me I know. I know. I know you know. I know you know I know.* They kiss. The word in Lucy's head is: *symmetry.* She does not know why. If she says it out loud, will she be understood again? Too much to ask? Opens her eyes and believes briefly she is looking in a mirror. Blinks. *Tell me what you're thinking.* And Dina swims back into focus, face assembling in the play of light. Lucy points. To OH 7. *What do we do?* The clinking. It's killing her. *What is it that he wants?*

There is a shrieking. The music swallowed. Wordless. Look. There, in the middle of the dance floor, the female *Homo habilis* on her knees. Keens—moans—bellows. On the floor the emptiness is shaped like the body of a child. She reaches for what isn't there. Above her, OH 7 clinking. The clinking is a crying. The dancers form a circle and point at the mourning mother. Point. Stare. Try to name her grief.

Exhibit: Piltdown Man

Several skull shards, half a lower jaw bearing a pair of molars, lifted from gravel pits in Sussex in 1908. The jaw, an apelike jaw. The teeth, worn in such a human way. A missing link. A revelation. The discoverer—Charles Dawson, local lawyer and amateur fossil collector. At the time of the discovery, forty-two and balding. But sporting a mustache of impressive volume.

It took forty-one years to reveal Piltdown as a fraud. The teeth, filed to flatness. The bones, a combination of human and orang-utan, less than a hundred years old, soaked in chromic acid and iron sulfate to simulate age.

Dear Charles Dawson, were you so middle-aged and sad? And to your colleagues, who latched onto your bones like drowning men to driftwood—did they want that badly for the earliest humans to be British? Gentlemen. I imagine you in your dark waistcoats, high white collars. I would like to be all condemnation. I would like to scold you for your lies, for fabricating an origin story to suit your needs. I would like to very much.

Back at the bar. How? She has not had *that* much to drink. Why can't she remember? And where is everyone? Dina, OH 7, the *Homo habilis* and her screams. The bartender asks can he get her anything. Lucy tries to say *No, thanks* but instead says, *Yes, please.* Scoop of ice into a cocktail shaker. Slush and clink of its contents. *Big night for you,* says the bartender. She frowns. *But it seems like a success!* Slides her the tumbler. *A new specialty. I call it the LUCA. Give it a taste.* The tumbler is empty.

She steps over the threshold and is overcome with mirrors. Far too many reflections. Too much bright light. They line the entryway on both sides and Lucy sees herself multiplied and split. A bit of the back of her head. The logo on her sneakers. Her cringe when the new foster mom swoops down with open arms. At least the dad just pats her on the shoulder. Awkward. Steps back. *And this is Danielle. She's your age. Call me Dani*, says Danielle. *I'm Lucy*, says Lucy. *Like* Peanuts? *What? Like in* Peanuts. *The cartoon.* The girl has a lot of dark hair, very glossy and straight. It's roped in two thick braids. She's skinny, like Lucy, and tall for her age—almost as tall as her mom. She wears Converse high tops and glasses. *Yeah*, says Lucy. *Like* Peanuts.

To the bartender, Lucy says, *I recently received some bad news.* She peers into the empty bottom of her tumbler. Its walls are cut with a pattern, in which the light refracts and magnifies. *I am slowly losing my ability to speak.* The bartender, wiping a glass, says, *Most myths about the beginnings of language are in fact about the beginnings of misunderstanding. Think of the Tower of Babel.* Lucy wishes her glass were not empty. Before her is a bowl holding lemon, orange, lime—swaths of missing peel, the pith bared like grazed skin. The etchings that decorate her glass look something like hieroglyphs, or like the wedges of cuneiform. She is convinced it is a language, but she cannot read it. *Or there's this tribe of Australian Aboriginals who believe the different languages arose when a group of their ancestors feasted on the body of a dead woman named Wurruri. Those who ate her flesh began to speak one language, those who ate her liver another, the intestines another. And so on and so on.* She realizes suddenly that the script on the glass is English. It spells out the name of the museum. *It has always been like this.*

Exhibit: Proto-world

The direct, genealogical predecessor of all existing languages. If the English word *human* comes from the Old French *humain*, and if *humain* comes from the Latin *humanus,* and if *humanus* comes from the Proto-Indo-European *dhghomon*—might not *dhghomon* come from a still earlier language, a language that once covered all the earth? Before Babel, was there a time when we all were bound?

But unlike the Last Universal Common Ancestor and unlike Mitochondrial Eve, Proto-World is purely hypothetical. Probably did not exist at all. Linguists attempt reconstructions, posit etymological paths, but go more than 5,000 years into the past and linguistic relationships become little more than conjecture. It is tempting, though, this single point of origin. This thing from which we all were birthed. Those things which existed at our origin must be those which are truest, and with this belief we burrow back, back, into the distant past, even when that past is gone forever. We imagine a history, we construct a taxonomy, an etymology, a genealogy, even if it is all a lie. We soak teeth in chromic acid, sift the soil for bones, create classifications and divisions—all in the hope of reaching a place beyond classification and division, a place from which every branch stems. After all, *dhghomon* comes from *dhghem*, meaning "earth," and everything on earth is what we seek to name.

One day, several months after moving in, Lucy pulls down her underwear to climb in the bath and sees them bloodied with brown. She sighs. Has been fearing this for months. Knew it was coming— an inevitability, its arrival nothing like shock. She tugs her jeans back on and goes down the hall to find her foster mom. *Funny,* she says, which is not the word Lucy would use. *Danielle got her first yesterday. She must have given it to you. Women are like that, you know.* Lucy does not know. Her foster mom hands her a pad. *Put this on after your bath. And keep yourself clean. Otherwise the smell is something like an animal.*

The family are Sunday churchgoers. Pentecostal. The building looks like a bad hotel lobby: fake plants, teal carpet, chintzy chandeliers. Her last family was Catholic, and the church was all statues and stained glass and wafers and wine. It delighted her. But there's none of that here. *Graven images,* her foster mother says. *God does not exist in objects.*

Lucy rakes a fingernail across the wooden lip of the pew. Studies the yellow grain. Next to her, Dani plays with her mother's watch, the links undulating like a snake. Snug silver scales. Rippling and released. Also the eyelash of a second hand, the tiny grooved knob for changing time, the catch and clasp that Dani latches and un-latches and latches again.

Dani looks up and sees Lucy watching. Holds out the watch in offering. Lucy opens a palm and the slinky silver thing drops in. Metal warm from manipulation.

At this moment, a shouting. A man two rows up and across the aisle, on his feet and shouting. Unintelligible sounds. Lucy stares in shock. Dani leans over. *Speaking in tongues,* she whispers. This means nothing to Lucy. From her position she cannot see the man's face, only the back of his head and a bit of his jaw, its muscles pumping and popping. The jawbone swinging on its hinge. There is a rhythm of language in the sounds and yet Lucy knows there can be no meaning in them. She wonders if this is god or the devil, and if neither god nor the devil then what it is exactly. So many heads face away from her, turned toward the man. She can see only the backs of their heads. Hair and neck and ears. The place on the men where the hair tapers off. Taut stretch of tendons below. And the women, even worse. So many masses of curls. Blonde brown black. Lucy tries to give them faces in her mind and cannot. The sounds coil and knot like ribbons in the air. How long will he go on like this, how long will everyone else wait, listening but kept forever outside? If this is speaking to god it is awful lonely, thinks Lucy.

The man falls shuddering back to his seat. The pastor into his microphone says, *Brothers and sisters, we have witnessed the gift of tongues here today.* In the bright metal of the watch, Lucy's face is not a face.

The party continues to rage. Lucy envies them. Their mouths open in a laughter she cannot hear. She scans the crowd for people speaking, but finds none. Mostly they are just moving in music. But there—in the throng, a couple trying to communicate. She cannot hear their voices over the noise, but she watches. The woman shouts to the man. The man shouts back, and without trying Lucy reads his lips: *What?* The woman shouting again, leaning in close, lips to his ear, and they do this back and forth for a while until each pulls back, nodding and smiling as if they have understood.

Where did you go? A shouting in her ear. Dina. *I lost you! I was here. I was here all along—I think. Well. Are you having fun?* A tinnitus suddenly crescendos in her ears. Ringing like a bad mic. *The others—they went on ahead. Come on, we have to catch up.* Dina's hand closes around hers and it feels good, to be held, to be led. The museum is arranged in rings. So far they have been in the outermost one, but now they head deeper inward. *It's time,* says Dina. *It's time to go the center. What's in the center?* asks Lucy. *Shhh,* says Dina.

Moving through museums always makes her anxious. The fear that she is missing something, or that she is going the wrong way. Once, on a high school field trip to the natural history museum, she found herself walking backward through a mass extinction event. *What do you think happened? Corpses bloated up like balloons and floated down the river. Or perhaps it was the poisoned drinking water, or perhaps they died elsewhere. Where they died. After which, larger predators, perhaps the* Allosaurus fragilis *(pronunciation: AL-*

oh-SORE-us fraj-ILL-iss), followed the stink of meat into the mire. And its tonnage pulled it under. Maybe a stegosaurus stumbled into a drying lake bed for a drink. But here are some are theories. No one knows. How did they get here? Over 12,000 specimens in a single location. We've got all these bones.

There is never just one way to go and she dislikes doubling back. Nowhere else can you move through time like this and she wishes to come out less disoriented, not more. But Dina must know the way. She moves decisively through the fossil glow, brownish light coming up from the displays. She says, *Most fossils form when the object itself is lost.* In the boxes of glass the bones are becoming less recognizable. Fewer faces and fingers and more knobs and shards. *Corpses decay and leave only their shapes behind.* The tinnitus still ringing, or is that simply silence? What can we know from the shape of a thing's lack? *Or minerals leak into organic matter, like wood and bone, and fill the empty spaces. We are full of empty spaces. Then the organic stuff goes and you get rock in the shape of cells.*

The farther they go the fainter the music. Only a trace of the beat remains. For the first time, Lucy hears the whisper of AC, like a sound from another world.

Exhibit: Debitage

The term *debitage* refers to the waste chips produced during lithic reduction, the tool-making procedures of prehistoric hominids. These flakes struck from stone may be able to tell us much about about our early ancestors, and the field of debitage analysis studies their mass, length, mid width, max width, platform length, platform width, bulb thickness, platform angle, platform configuration, platform facet count, percent dorsal cortex, dorsal scar count, remained portion, size grade, source location, and so on. In other words, there is much to read in the shape of a rock.

This exhibit, however, does not attempt to sort or analyze its debitage. Rather, the debitage is arranged in heaps upon the floor, so that you may walk through and around it. This exhibit is okay to touch! Try rolling in the chips, try lifting them in handfuls and letting them fall. Try fitting chips together and seeing what absence they form.

The flakes roll in pale waves around her. They rise high in places, higher than her head, heaping up almost to the ceiling. They bloom and swell, they eddy and churn. *Termites pulped the boxes and the obsidian streamed. Oh Mary Mary m a r y M A R Y.* Flaked pieces, detached pieces, pounded pieces, unmodified pieces. *I'm sure that an autobiography, like any other book, needs a structure to hold it together.* In the archives too the papers formed a sea. Perhaps a museum is a charnel ground. Perhaps it's all a long sick joke. Perhaps this curve and crack of rock is no alphabet at all. *Try rolling in the chips!* But she cannot bring herself to touch.

I have a soft spot for this particular gallery, admits Dina, among the shapeless fossils and chips of waste. *It makes me feel such a stupid rush of love. For our species, I mean. Our dumb, frightened, desperate species. I mean look at all the things that we will keep!* She gestures to the heaped debris. *We are such gluttons for myth.*

Lucy on the other hand feels a strange sadness. The scope of it all, the heap of rock, the depth of time. There's a claustrophobia too, a fear that these pale shards will descend on her, devour her like teeth. *Let's go,* she says, and heads for the gallery's exit, quick, quick, before she begins to cry.

EXHIBIT: GEOFACTS OF THE CALICO HILLS

Study these stones. Do they look to you like tools? These chipped flints and cherts, discovered in the Mojave Desert's Calico Hills, do appear much like artifacts produced in the Oldowan or Acheulean tool-making traditions. Scientists such as Louis Seymour Bazett Leakey claimed they were 100,000-year old tools, evidence of human activity in the Americas some five times earlier than the generally accepted date. But such theories were quickly discredited. *Of course there were flakes of chert incorporated in the deposit,* said Louis's wife, Mary, who found his Calico work an embarrassment. *In such circumstances, how could there fail to be?*

Geofact: a naturally occurring stone object that is difficult to distinguish from a human artifact. Look at them, their oblong shapes, pointed tips, flaked sides. Don't you want to believe they exist for hands like yours?

Oh Mary Mary Mary Mary. You watched him, old and sick, digging in the hills. His sweat cut rivulets down his dirt-dark skin, his spine cracked and groaned when he rose. You were embarrassed. You parted ways. But for a moment, didn't you almost believe?

Beyond the ring of shapeless fossils and unknowable stones is a third ring. They stand at its entrance and Dina nudges Lucy forward. *You go on.* She does. The ring at first seems empty. Just as she begins to search, there is a scream behind her. Lucy jumps and whirls around. *What? What?* But it's only Dina, laughing. Holding her stomach and laughing. *What is it?* But she just keeps laughing.

EXHIBIT: SIGNALING THEORY

Perhaps language evolved from animal communication. Washoe the chimpanzee, Koko the gorilla, Kanzi the bonobo—all apes who communicate, memorizing hundreds of signs or symbols and even sometimes constructing rudimentary grammar. *You can have some cereal if you give Austin your monster mask to play with,* Kanzi's trainer said to him during a visit with Austin the chimpanzee. Kanzi retrieved the mask, handed it to Austin, then pointed at the cereal. Even dolphins can learn to communicate using an underwater keyboard, and Alex the grey parrot could answer questions about color, shape, number, and size with 80% accuracy.

So perhaps animals do have the cognitive capacity for language. But the problem is not so much cognitive or anatomical. The problem is that words are cheap. Signals sent by animals must be intrinsically reliable. They must be costly to produce, difficult to falsify. The young springbok, for instance, signals its youth by leaping into the air, back arched, legs stiff, head pointing down—a signal that tells predators, *I am not worth chasing.* The Eurasian jay squawks to let the fox know, *I see you. You will be unable to surprise me.* And so the fox gives up. The crested anole lizard performs push-ups to inform the mongoose of its fitness, scaly little arms pumping an irrefutable truth. The mongoose wanders off. Energy is saved, for both predator and prey.

Exhibit: Chimpanzee vocalizations and gestures

Roar-pant, hoot-hoot, arrival pant-hoot, inquiring pant, spontaneous pant-hoot, bark, waa-bark, cough, hoo, huu, food grunt, food aaa, copulation scream, whimper, squeak, victim scream, tantrum scream, SOS scream, crying, pant-grunt, pant-bark, pant-scream, pant, soft grunt, extended grunt, copulation pant, nest grunt, laughter, wraah.

Arm-on, arm-raise, back-offer, ball-offer, belly-offer, direct-hand, foot-stomp, genital-offer, ground-slap, hand-beg, hand-clap, head-bob, head-shake, lead, leg-offer, lip-lock, look-back, point, poke-at, push-object, raise-object, reach, rub-chin, shake-object, spit-at, swagger, throw-stuff, touch-side, wave-object, wrist-offer.

(...subject approaches the other with its arm extended and places its arm on the other's back. Subject presents ball to the other, taking it back to invite wrestling. Subject puts the other's hands in its own. Subject slaps ground and looks to the other. Subject rapidly shakes head horizontally at the other. Subject runs away, looking over its shoulder at the other. Subject pushes an object in the other's direction. Subject strokes chin of the other and looks to its face....)

Exhibit: Vervet monkey alarm calls

The predators of the vervet monkey include snakes, hawks, leopards, and baboons. Like many animals, vervets will emit a cry to signal the presence of a predator. A warning to their kin. But what's interesting about vervets is their ability to emit a *different* signal for each of their four predators (press the buttons below to hear each one!). In this sense, the cries are not just emotionally induced, like a scream or a gasp. They are *referential.* They refer to specific objects. Does this not meet the requirement for language—a rudimentary language, a language that points?

But the cries still only occur in the presence of a predator. Whereas humans routinely use words in the absence of their referents. Can you point to what isn't there?

The vervets' inability to control their vocalizations means they are unable to fake them. Deception is impossible: the signals can be trusted. Consider Jane Goodall's chimpanzee, who discovered a cache of bananas and wanted to keep them for himself. Unable to prevent the instinctual pant-hoot indicating the discovery of food, he nevertheless attempted to muffle it by placing his hand over his mouth. Nor could the pant-hoot ever be produced in the *absence* of food. This is not language. This is not language precisely *because* it is so fused to the world, to what is right at hand.

EXHIBIT: SIMA DE LOS HUESOS, ATAPUERCA, SPAIN
(REVISITED)

So how could language like ours evolve? It is a Darwinian impossibility. Language, divorced from its referent, holds no weight. Fiction poses problems for any species dependent on language.

The theory goes that language could not have evolved without a larger culture of symbolic meaning. Cultural institutions, religious ritual, mythology, the rule of law—these things needed to exist to give words weight. A new order of reality was required for words to work.

And so we are back to our Pit of Bones. Back to the forty-three-foot vertical shaft, the 6,000 hominid fossils piled in a heap, the pink hand ax like some flower, blooming. We are back to sentences about things that do not exist.

And then she is alone again. All hint of music, gone. An empty gallery. Clean white walls waiting for something to hold. An anonymous sound of air moving in vents and a carpet she has seen before. She cannot hear her own breathing. Goes from feeling haunted to wishing she were haunted. The emptiness of this place holds no trace of the dead. It frightens her more than any ghost.

Summer. Naperville, Illinois. The heat coming down fast and hot and humid. There is heat that hangs and there is heat that beats and this is a heat that beats. Asphalt scars on the road, like some strange calligraphy, and the DuPage River a larger scar. Its water dark and snaking, the trees throwing their green-black light. Near the river, what was once a limestone quarry has been converted into a swimming facility. The shallows the color of spearmint. Visitors enter slowly. Water ascends their bodies and there is a smell of sunscreen and chlorine. Deeper, deeper, and they can feel a cool rising up from the depths, like cool white lime. They imagine the bright terrace of the mine, its tornado shape opening up the land. Imagine the men in overalls and wide-brimmed hats, men sweaty with dust sticking to the sweat, men with sledgehammers arcing hard against rock, splitting the rock along its seams, pluming further dust into their hair and eyes and lungs. Or they think of none of this, because the day is so hot and there are thick loud crowds in the water and the sun is melting like an ice cream cone above them. There are box stores along Highway 59 and crosswalks striping the streets and baseball diamonds with soft combed dirt. All of this is Naperville. And two blocks down from the former quarry, two twelve-year-old girls wander the Naperville Historical Museum, which boasts twenty-six buildings from the city's origins. A hotel and tavern, a smithy, a print shop. A lone outhouse from the 1860s, which some children might giggle at, but which elicits frowns from these two girls. The absurdity strikes them simultaneously—that this is what has been preserved. *How long do you think our toilet will last,* asks one, and they mentally catalogue all their belongings, thinking suddenly of these items as artifacts. Their books and clothes, the dollhouse they are already too old for, the violin, the Game Boy, the soccer ball and cleats, the hula hoop. Where will such objects end up? In one hundred years, what will rot in a landfill and what will be preserved under glass?

Dina with a notebook in her lap. Scribbling. *It's wrong, it's wrong, it's all all wrong.* Tapes her papers to the wall, tears them down again. *I am leaving so much out and making so much up.*

Point. Point. Point at nothing. Try—impossible. Point and you will always point at something. It is a foolish reason to feel joy— that you cannot point at nothing—but joy is what she feels.

You cannot point at nothing. But can you point at what isn't there?

True fact, says Dina. *Museum visitors, on average, spend two seconds looking at the exhibit, ten seconds reading the label, look briefly back at the exhibit, then move on. There was a study. Used cameras to track their gaze. Do you see what I'm saying?* Lucy is afraid she does. She's saying: what's in the box doesn't matter. She's saying: the box could very well be empty. She's saying: Not only is it *possible* to point at what isn't there—that's all we ever do.

Old Naper Settlement again. A summer storm rolls in and traps them in the chapel. Alone, they sit cross-legged in front of the altar. Rain spatters the stained glass. Prickles the rooftop. *It's haunted, you know,* says Dani. Lucy can see her face reflected in the other girl's glasses. Focuses alternately on her reflection in the lenses and on the eyes behind them. Tries to see both at once, but it's impossible. *Ghosts of dead quarrymen and factory workers and ghosts of murdered angry Indians. Ghosts from the great and awful train crash of 1946. Have you heard of that? You haven't? Two trains smashed right into each other. Train cars everywhere like little toys. Screams from people dying and bleeding. The whole city smelled like oil and ash and burnt dead bodies for days. No for months! Anyway, the ghosts are here now and if you look real close you can still see their clothes smoking.* A bray of thunder. Low and loud. *Nice story,* says Lucy, who is old enough to know she should not be scared of ghost talk. *What?* says Dani. *You don't believe in ghosts?* A bright snap of lightning outside the window. *No.* The lightning. It's supposed to come first. She must have missed something. She waits for the crack of thunder. Listens close and hard and far, far off, believes she hears a whistle. Long like a moan. *Well you should.*

Dina rips text from wall. The words falling at her feet. Lucy says, *Stop!* Collage of overlapping language: *they trail red soft hot ash a lineage of this space between like an offering a conchoidal fracture million years To point mandible with gloved bones sinking thy sorrow and chromic acid Try as we might the deepest slots Follow my accuse, appoint, declare murky with time*

Stop stop stop.

Going home and there is a smell of rain on the pavement. Water warming in the weak small sun. *Want to go back tomorrow?* asks Dani. Lucy dodges the worms scattered on the sidewalk, their bodies plump from rainwater. *We've been every day this week,* she says. *Don't you like it?* says Dani. *Sure I like it. But we've seen everything already. So? So—hey!* Lucy stops abruptly. Dani has just stomped hard on the body of an earthworm, her sneaker spreading its guts across the path. *What'd you do that for?* Dani turns and looks at her. *It was half crushed already. I kill the dying ones. It's kinder.* The two girls stare at each other. Lucy looks for her face in Dani's glasses; it is not there. *I don't want to go to the museum again. You can go.* Around them there is a sound of dripping. A slight steam lifts from the street. *Fine,* says Dani. *I will.*

Lucy and Dina sitting cross-legged on the floor. Near them, the antelope bone in its glass. *What?* says Dina. *You don't believe in ghosts?*

EXHIBIT: ANTELOPE METAPODIAL BONE (REVISITED)

There are ninety-one species of antelope. Perhaps this bone comes from an impala or a gazelle. Perhaps wildebeest or kudu. Perhaps the giant eland, largest of the antelope, weighing up to 2,000 pounds. Antelope is a wastebasket taxon—a category for that which fits nowhere else. What is an antelope? An antelope is not a cow. Not a sheep. Not a buffalo, a bison, a goat. *Incertae sedis.* Of uncertain placement. Known by what it is not.

Exhibit: Antelope metapodial bone (revisited)

Beyond our reach. The protohumans (male) reaching out to seize upon this prize. The pooling blood, the meat revealing its ribbons. The greater kudu of eastern and southern Africa can be found grazing in the scrubby woodlands. The males of the species possess great twisting horns, slanting back slightly from the skull, with which they sometimes spar—locking horns together and shoving. Sometimes the horns lock so tightly they cannot come undone. The animals trapped in a vice of bone. Face to face, wild eyed. Frantic until they die.

The scream enters her dream before it wakes her. She dreams she is standing by a train track watching two trains hurtle toward each other. She opens her mouth to scream, but nothing comes out. Stands with her mouth wide and empty as the two trains collide and unfurl a thick quilt of smoke over the earth. Flame turns grass to tinder. From one train stumbles a woman, her body on fire, eyes bloodred and wild. She looks not quite human. She screams and the scream jolts Lucy awake. Her bedroom is bright with late morning sun and the scream is still going. It's coming from downstairs. She blinks, rubs her eyes, but cannot seem to clear the sleep from her vision. It's her foster mom screaming. Lucy stumbles from the room and down the stairs, everything still blurry. Turns the corner into the living room and sees a bright rectangle of daylight. The front door open. And in the rectangle is a dark shape. She blinks again. The shape is that of a man. He's in a police officer's uniform. His face is little more than a smudge but his posture is like a grimace. And in front of him, still in her dressing gown, there is a woman. On her knees, screaming.

Exhibit: Antelope metapodial bone (revisited)

A child points to the museum exhibit, asks his mother, *What's that?* A graduate student in a brightly lit lab points to a striation, says, *Evidence of butchery.* At an excavation site in east Africa, a researcher points and exclaims, *Look!* The bone pokes from the stripped earth. Go back two million years. The bone lies at the center of a ring of protohumans who point and say nothing and everything at once.

Exhibit: Antelope metapodial bone (revisited)

The woody grain, like a tree limb. Joints, slightly worn. Imagine them grating, bulb of one bone against the crater of the next. Like a pestle scraping the mortar's bowl. Chafing again and again as the long legs of this beast carry it swift across the plain. White belly, black stripe along the flank. Ribbed horns curving slightly back. In humans, the metapodial bones are in the hands and feet, but in quadrupeds they form the lower limb. What you think is the elbow is actually the wrist.

EXHIBIT: ANTELOPE METAPODIAL BONE (REVISITED)

You would like to touch it, I know. But you cannot.

Exhibit: Antelope metapodial bone (revisited)

And how did the creature die? A cheetah, possibly, or a leopard, a lion, hyena. It zigzagged through grass but not fast enough. And after the cat's maw was pinked with blood, its belly distended with flesh, it loped off to lick its whiskers somewhere cool and shady. And the corpse lay waiting to become something else.

Dina cross-legged on the floor, a bloody mass of animal in her lap. Has a blade and is scissoring away its skin, lifting it from muscle like a pale glossy peel. Connective tissue stretches like cellophane. Blood vessels bulge. Around her are skeletons of wire and wool. A hundred antelope forms waiting for their skins. She tugs hard on the hide. Pulling it inside out. *The skin is like a sleeping bag or a glove,* she says. A smudge of blood on her face. Down to the hooves now, peeling the skin right past the cloven toes. She grunts as she rips. Another leg then another and another. Next the head. Pulling the skin over it like some slick turtleneck. *Now I will cut carefully around the eyes so as to preserve the lashes and lids.* Inside the head of the animal is another head, this one slippery and red. She cuts carefully, face so close her nose brushes blood. Then with a final slice the lips come off and the whole hide is free. She brandishes it back like a drawn curtain. The form in her lap fetal and raw. The skin dripping from her fist.

She fits the pelt around the mannequin, tugs it tight like pulling on jeans. From her pocket she draws needle and thread. *What is an antelope?* she asks, and begins to stitch.

The funeral, a bright blistering day. A boy lifting mounds of damp dirt. The pastor speaking about angels. Lucy remembers the first day at the museum. She had never been to a place like that before, had never been confronted with so much history. Staring at a glass case of silver spoons. Hundreds. Each labeled with a name and date and she became sick and dizzy. Heart going too fast. A hundred sewing machines. A hundred teacups. A hundred empty chairs. The names and dates. The names and dates. Mannequins in hoop skirts and crinoline—fake hair but no faces. Glass and more glass, every surface a reflection. All these dead and this is what remains of them. A thousand daguerreotype eyes. A morsel of horsemeat, turned long ago to fossil. A braided swatch of hair. A miner's carriage lamp, a lump of iron ore, several dozen baby prams, brass knuckles, muskets. An exhibit for keys without locks and locks without keys, for railroad ties and tobacco pipes, for every single surviving shoe. A taxidermied lamb. The first bag of sugar. Roomful of children's toys, such ghostly circus colors. What things to keep. And this is what she thinks of now, with the heat ramming its way through the trees, with the heavy square of sod being pressed back into place. The sod is inches thick and the sound it makes when moved is a meaty sound.

Lucy wanders the gallery as Dina prepares her specimens. The ones she's finished stare with eyes of glass. Arranged in various lifelike poses: midair leap or neck bent to graze. Each with its name affixed: springbok, hartebeest, klipspringer, dik-dik. Fake rock and fake grasses, the walls painted with blue and cloud. A giant eland on a ledge, its mouth open. A fake tongue disappears into the black illusion of a throat. The stiff jaw. The dark lips. Plastic glistening as if with saliva. Lucy stands staring into this dark animal mouth. The cave of it. Mandible a useless hanging hinge. And she believes suddenly not just in the existence of its throat, but that its throat continues eternally, unending chasm, that she could insert a hand into this ungulate's gaping mouth and lose it there forever. The parted lips. The stony tongue. The small flattish teeth. She squints and peers but can make out nothing. No back to this mouth. And there is a mounting horror.

In the chapel when the storm rolls in. Outside, the lift and groan of thunder, the clouds bearing down and sweeping the land with rain. *Well you should.* The girl smiling at her and then leaning in. Her mouth tastes like mustard from their lunch.

Her foster mom on the floor. The officer's face refusing to come into focus. She will think about this for years, how his face remained blurred to her, and she will wonder what she might have seen there. Genuine compassion? Feigned sympathy? Discomfort, embarrassment at this woman's naked pain? Or perhaps nothing. An implacable, professional calm.

The usual lobby furnishings. Vinyl armchairs and pastel walls. A plant in the corner she gives a twenty percent chance of being real. On the table, magazines. Fanned out and overlapping, so that half of each cover is obscured by the next. She waits. Eventually, the door opens and she is ushered into the office. Her foster parents look at her with faces wordless and wide. *We're here today because your parents are worried about you.* Her foster dad nods. He appears nervous. But in her foster mom's face is something different: a hard still stare. Transfixed. Boring into Lucy's face as if in it is something she desperately needs.

Do you see her now? Where is she? Point! Point to where she is!

Beside Dina on the floor, a pile of fake tongues. Pinkish, blackish. And the eyeballs, their skewed pupils roiling.

EXHIBIT: ANTELOPE METAPODIAL BONE (REVISITED)

To point is to touch what you cannot. The circle of large dark eyes, desire mirrored everywhere. How much of life consists of craving. And how much of fear. The protohumans watching each other. Careful and close. The clearing brims with hunger and the stink of meat. In their bodies is the urge to fight, to kill, to do whatever it takes to possess this carcass. Never before has a species posed such a risk to itself. Never has a species *wanted* this fiercely.

And so the sign is offered. Violence is deferred, and if this happens once it will happen again and again. The sign repeated, pointing to objects of desire in order to speak about them, and in speaking, survive.

To point is to share a world with another. To point is to direct another's gaze. To say *Look!* and believe they might see what you see. To point is to love. It is to touch what you cannot and lose what you might have held.

And now Dina is stitching a real bone into the leg of a specimen. Tiny holes at the bone's edge, through which she threads her needle. Bone dust and a drill on the floor. *Should you be doing that?* asks Lucy. *To reassemble history is our task*, Dina replies. She sews faster, needle going in great loops. The animal she has chosen is pure white and the empty hide takes the shape of a ghost. Its discarded body off to one side. *The springbok,* says Dina, not looking up, *is the sole member of the genus* Antidorcas, *which is derived from the Greek "anti," meaning opposite, and "dorcas," meaning gazelle. The springbok is an antelope that is not a gazelle. The antelope is an ungulate that is not a cow. All this negative taxonomy.* She stops sewing. Looks up, nose still bloody. *That was good. Write that down, will you?*

EXHIBIT: WHITE SPRINGBOK WITH INCORPORATED METAPODIAL BONE

The springbok is the sole member of the genus *Antidorcas*, which is derived from the Greek "anti," meaning opposite, and "dorcas," meaning gazelle. The springbok is an antelope that is not a gazelle. The antelope is an ungulate that is not a cow. All this negative taxonomy. *Taxonomy* translates as "arrangement of names," while *taxidermy* is "arrangement of skin." A species whose genus was created specifically to classify it is considered a *sui generis* species. *Sui generis*: of its own kind. *Incertae sedis:* of uncertain placement—used for names that cannot be placed in the current taxonomic scheme. Isolated, lacking genealogy and history. A whole language to describe the failures of this naming. Not to mention that the pure white springbok has been artificially selected by South African ranchers. A subspecies without a past. Strange home for this old bone.

Where is she. Point. So Lucy does. Lifts an arm. Points. Her foster mom spins to face the designated corner. Lets out a small noise: *oh.* Approaches the space. Drops to her knees. *Oh my baby.*

Why. Why did you tell. *She misses you.* You know I'm not real. *She misses you so much.* You know it and you lied. *Maybe you are real. You seem real.* I am a thing of your mind. You know it and you lied.

No sooner is the bone secure in its new body than Dina cries and tears it back out. There is a sound of snapping threads like something being popped from a socket. The animal's skin hangs frayed and loose from its leg. Dina weeps, cradles the bone to her chest like a child. Lucy opens her mouth to say, *What are you doing?* but instead there is only a snarl. Her lips curl back and she bares her teeth. The image of Dina with the bone, holding it, owning it—she lunges. She seizes Dina's head in her hands and rips at the long dark braids. She claws at Dina's face, leaves thin blood down her cheeks, like tracks cut by tears. Dina throws the bone, grabs Lucy's face in return and digs thumbs into eyeballs. Feels the soft orbs below the lids. Feels the way she could push down, press and pop, feels the way this is just another skin to be peeled from the body. Feels something in her throat, rising to fill her mouth. It is a scream. A hundred miles off, in the Appalachians, a pair of white-tailed deer rot on the forest floor. Their antlers locked, their eye sockets inches apart, they are mirror images of bone. Like the pair of bucks in Ohio, pair of bull moose in the Yukon, pair of kudu in Botswana. Antlered together, face to face, frantic until they die. Such lethal symmetry. And the two women in this museum that is a discotheque. Faces close enough they might fuse and merge, might become one. But at the same time, what distance is between them, what unbridgeable gap. How Lucy can sometimes see herself in these eyes, a bulged reflection, but can never see herself *through* these eyes. Can never look out from behind them. How Dina is never more than surface to her. The whole world, a mere collection of surfaces.

EXHIBIT: THE SURFACE OF LAKE TURKANA

That's right, just the surface, thin blue film peeled away like the skin of an apple and transported here for your enjoyment. Surface reveals shape: long and skinny and ever so slightly curved, like a mackerel lifting its tail. You'll notice holes, like cigarette burns in fabric. Those are the islands, volcanic calderas opening into perfect brown bowls. The islands are cratered and the craters fill with water, forming miniature Lake Turkanas inside the larger one. What tattered cloth. Go ahead, touch it, feel its liquid barely there. Afterward, lick your fingers: salt and alkaline. Potable, but not anything you'd want to drink. A couple million years ago, though, early humans flocked to the lake in droves. How many skeletons were swallowed by its banks, bones sinking in the brackish soil? For instance the mass grave on the southern shore, where the remains of twenty-seven early humans were discovered with arrow tips lodged in thoraces and skulls. Head bones, rib bones, leg bones, bashed in by some blunt force. Imagine being the anthropologist who discovered this, while searching, maybe, for what it means to be human. Imagine lifting so many battered bodies into the light. Another. Another. Dusting chalky soil from their wounds. Truthfully, these weren't "early" humans at all; the remains are just 10,000 years old. These were sapiens.

And what, after all, can a surface tell us? Shape, texture, taste. And? Where does surface end? At what point does outside become inside? Maybe the problem is we didn't get it all—should have gone several molecules deeper. Leaving the lake, we looked behind us.

Saw another surface already formed like a fresh blue skin. Skin is surface—is the largest human organ. If you know my skin do you know me? Skin is where I meet the world. Humans think to see the surface of an object is to see the object. This is possibly true in the case of a soap bubble. Certainly untrue in the case of a mirror. The sun appears to have a surface but it doesn't; it's all gas, and the place where heat and light become their opposites is like the place where waking becomes sleep. The surface of the earth is 197 million square miles. Peel it back to find the mantle and core and all that they hold. Maybe next time we'll bring back the depth instead. Long blue rod, 358 feet at its deepest point. Maybe this could tell us more.

We're here today because your parents are worried about you. Her foster mom's face: a hard still stare. *You know Danielle is dead.* Boring into her face as if—*Yes. I know. But you've been seeing her around?* Lucy nods. As if in it there is something other than a face. Other than *her* face. *Do you see her now? Where is she?* Lucy points.

In the days after the funeral the house is full of flowers and stillness and summer light. The neighbors come over to clean and leave the linoleum in the kitchen spotless and sad. Her foster mom locked in her bedroom, her foster dad out who knows where, Lucy sits on the living room couch with her knees to her chest. Watches the sun move from noon to dusk. Through the windows, the long yellow light coming in columns. Stretching itself out along the carpet, stretching the shadows cast from table and chairs. A final bright spear and the sun slips away.

Lucy feels emptied. Her mind capable of holding nothing. She forgets the day, the year, her face, her name. Forgets who or what she is. Lifts her hands before her eyes and stares and stares. Time has become the strangest thing. *Ten days*, she reminds herself, but the phrase holds no meaning. It does not feel like ten days, though it feels neither longer nor shorter. Time moves around her but does not carry her with it.

The night darkens until the windows become panes of reflected light, the world beyond obscured. Lucy stands and walks to Dani's room. Surveys the objects in the dark. Clothes hanging in the closet, shadowy, cold, the torsos of ghosts. Soiled clothes in the hamper. She lifts a sweater and can smell the dead girl on it. Removes her own shirt and pulls the sweater over her head, feels a loosening in her body, akin to letting out a sigh. Pulls out a pair of jeans. Discards her own and tugs these on. She's grown enough in the past six months that she and Dani are nearly the same height. The clothes fit her well. She looks down at her body and is convinced she is not herself. Dani's viewing. The corpse in the casket, looking like a doll. And now it is sunk in the earth, and Lucy cannot stop thinking about the way it will decay, the skin shrinking and retreating, becoming pocked by holes, the holes growing and spreading until there is no flesh left for holes to open. And then the shape of her unbound bones—an illegible script of vertebrae and rib.

Lucy looks up and in the corner sees a face. Thinks for a moment she is looking in a mirror. But there is no mirror.

Exhibit: Glossolalia with Adam and Eve

gatacca cacc atga acttaac tatata gatgat atacaga And god said *tagaca tagaca tat* And god said *atga cataca* And, behold, it was very good *taaga gat cacaga ta* Word that created thee, and against which thou hast transgressed *ataca ataga tact* The archangel Jophiel going to the garden *tagtaca taca agt a a a* Adam's naked cock and balls and Eve's naked breasts *gatacca gat agat tacata aca tac* And the Lord God brought them unto Adam to see what he would call them *tccc tcc tca* And whatsoever Adam called every living creature, that was the name thereof *atg acg a* And Adam called his wife's name Eve; because she was the mother of all living *gatc atcg* Jophiel, Jophiel will you teach us your language? *atcg gata acta* A pure language of the angels, the purest form of prayer *gatc ctga tgac* Jophiel draws a sword of flame and Eve and Adam weep *gatc atcg tcga cagt* A man two rows up and across the aisle, on his feet and shouting *catacagata tca* She can see only the backs of their heads *tacatacatac* The jawbone swinging on its hinge *gattacagattaca* If this is speaking to god it is awful lonely *gatc gatc gatcata cact* And the angel Jophiel cast them from the garden *tatagcatat* And God ceased to commune with them

And now the final ring. Its edge forms the lip of a great caldera, its bowl bluing with morning and with mist. They descend its cupped slopes, advance across, headed for the center. Bones litter the soil. *There.* Pointing. She looks. *He's over there.* In the grass, the small pile of him. Mandible, teeth, parietal. Finger, hand, wrist. And somewhere far off across the blue caldera, she knows a *Homo habilis* woman roams the land searching for her son. The woman on the cusp of becoming human. If she can only find him.

The face in the corner comes into focus and it is Dani's face. *You're dead*, says Lucy. *But not gone,* says the face. Lucy stares. Then turns, exits, slams the door behind her.

Exhibit: Linguistic recursion

I know. I know that you know. I know that you know that I know. I know that you know that I know that you know. I know that you know that I know that you know that I know. I know that you know that I know that you know that I know that you know. I know that you know that I know that you know that I know that you know that I know. I know that you know that I know that you know that I know that you know that I know. I know that you know that I know that you know that I know that you know that I know that you know that I know. I know that you know that I know that you know that I know that you know that I know that you know that I know. I know that you know that I know that you know that I know that you know that I know that you know that I know that you know that I know that you know. I know that you know that I know that you know that I know that you know that I know that you know that I know that you know that I know. I know that you know that I know that you know that I know that you know that I know that you know that I know that you know that I know that you know. I know that you know that I know that you know that I know that you know that I know that you know that I know that you know that I know. I know that you know that I know that you know that I know that you know that I know that you know that I know that you know that I know that you know that I know. I know that you know that I know that you know that I know that you know that I know that you know that I know that you know that I know that you know that I know that you know that I know that you know. I know that you know that I know that you know that I know that you know that I know that

you know that I know that you know that I know that you know
that I know that you know that I know that you know. I know
that you know that I know that you know that I know that you
know that I know that you know that I know that you know that
I know that you know that I know that you know that I know that
you know that I know. I know that you know that I know that you
know that I know that you know that I know that you know that
I know that you know that I know that you know that I know that
you know that I know that you know that I know that you know.
I know that you know that I know that you know that I know that
you know that I know that you know that I know that you know
that I know that you know that I know that you know that I know
that you know that I know that you know that I know. I know
that you know that I know that you know that I know that you
know that I know that you know that I know that you know that
I know that you know that I know that you know that I know that
you know that I know that you know that I know that you know.
I know that you know that I know that you know that I know that
you know that I know that you know that I know that you know
that I know that you know that I know that you know that I know
that you know that I know that you know that I know that you
know that I know. I know that you know that I know that you
know that I know that you know that I know that you know that I
know that you know that I know that you know that I know that
you know that I know that you know that I know that you know
that I know that you know that I know that you know.

Lucy, Dina, OH 7, lying in the long grass. A swarm of tsetse flies and a wildebeest's bellow. The air over the horizon watery with mirage. *Is this real?* asks Lucy. Dina laughs. *Of course it isn't real.* OH 7 is still and small. Almost lost in the green-brown brushstrokes of the savannah. *Well it's an impressive reconstruction.* The place seems miles large and eons old. Dina sighs. *But not what I wished. It falls short.* A pause, in which the white sun appears to rotate slowly on its axis. *Do you think she will find us?* asks Lucy. Dina sighs once more and in the sound there is the sadness of years. Tears appear in Lucy's eyes. She reaches out and, for the first time, touches OH 7. Slides a soft finger across the black and glossy crowns of his teeth. *One two three four five six seven eight nine ten eleven twelve thirteen.* Incisors imperfectly aligned. The little rift valleys in his molars. Her tears spill. The closer to the beginning they get, the farther away they feel. Either the past is lost or it is painfully close.

Exhibit: Mitochondrial Eve of the genus *Homo*

A nameless river at the bottom of a gorge. She can look into the water and recognize the reflection is hers. She can wade into the current and feel its cold rush on her skin. She is pregnant, belly taut and large under her dark pelt, nipples swollen and breasts heavy. Eve was not named until after the Fall—known in the Garden only as *woman*. Like Eve, this woman too does not have a name. Like Eve, she will mother all the earth, like Eve bear many children and like Eve lose a son. Eve discovering the body of Abel. The first mourning, first mother to mourn a child. *I will greatly multiply thy sorrow and thy conception; in sorrow thou shalt bring forth children.* Mitochondrial Eve is not necessarily the first female member of a species; she is merely the most recent female ancestor from which the whole species descends. She had sisters, aunts, cousins. Hundreds of others whose lineages faded out. She is remarkable only because of all that is gone, all the sorrow and death that surrounds her. Again: what is lost always forms the boundary of what is.

Home again after the therapist's visit. Her foster dad has retreated to the back patio with a bottle of scotch. Her foster mom heats a can of soup for the two of them to share. They sit at the table without eating, the steam coming up in spectral curls. Her foster mom's name is Danielle also. A name she no longer wants to say out loud. Danielle stares glazed and vacant into her soup. The skin of her face sags, makeup-less and tired. *Behold, I show you a mystery,* she mutters. *We shall not all sleep, but we shall all be changed.* She looks up suddenly at Lucy and Lucy looks back, unsure. *1 Corinthians 15:51. Do you know what it means?* Lucy shakes her head. The look in the woman's eyes is now a look too fierce to name. It is frenzy and grief and hope and desire. *The dead are never gone, Lucy. What you have experienced these weeks—it isn't illness or hallucination.* She pauses, staring so hard Lucy wants to look away, but doesn't. *Do you see her now?* Lucy doesn't, but she knows this is the wrong answer. So she nods. *Where?* Moment of hesitation. *Where is she? Point!* So Lucy does. Lifts an arm. Points.

Come on, says Lucy, wiping a hand across her cheek to dry it. *Let's keep going.* Dina rolls onto her stomach, face down in the dirt. *But it's so hot,* she groans. *And I am so tired.* Lucy stands. Bruises are already blooming on her arms and neck, from where Dina grabbed her, and the scratches on Dina's face still seep with blood. *We have to keep going. We have to reach the center.* Dina rolls over again and squints up at Lucy. *Why? When did this become a journey and what are we journeying toward?* Lucy frowns. She has no immediate reply. *You built this place. Don't you know? I know what you know,* answers Dina, and she rolls back over. Lucy huffs. Bends and scoops OH 7 into her hands. *Well we're going. You can come or not.* She walks several paces off, and when she looks back, Dina is gone.

Far off across the blue caldera, the *Homo habilis* woman roams the land, searching for her son.

Dressed in the dead girl's clothes, sitting on the dead girl's floor, the dead girl's mother behind her on the bed. Long slow strokes of the hairbrush. *Ask Dani if she wants two braids or one.* It has been many weeks since Lucy last saw Dani, but she speaks to her, on her foster mom's behalf, every day. *She says two, please.* School has started but she has not gone. *And what would Dani like for dinner tonight?* Lucy has stopped hearing her own name spoken. She hears only the name *Dani,* and when she replies, *Dani would like chicken noodle soup, please,* she feels as if she is speaking of herself in the third person. There is no Dani. There is only Lucy, imagining, constructing, projecting another. She feels lonelier than ever.

Lucy wanders in the tall grass and brownish sedge. *When did this become a journey and what are we journeying toward?* She tries to ask OH 7 about his life, his death, but the words are leaking from her faster now. *Most likely a genetic component.* She wonders about her parents, her grandparents, wonders if they too lost the command of language. Lived in skulls thick with words, crowded with them, but lacked all ability to bring what was inside out. She has wished her whole life for some tether to her ancestors—perhaps this is it. Perhaps her connection with them is isolation, is this grey matter jail cell. What good is language that is only internal. Language that swirls and spirals, the cadence of thought, but can never break out, never enter the world, never touch people and rocks and trees. What good is glossolalia, speaking in tongues no earthly being speaks.

She heads for what she thinks is the center of the caldera, the center of the museum. What will she find there? What if she finds nothing? A glass box, empty. Or perhaps holding—

Exhibit: AL 288-1

A girl with kaleidoscope eyes.

Exhibit: AL 288-1

Archangel Jophiel, going to the garden. Adam's naked cock and balls and Eve's naked breasts. *Adam called his wife's name Eve; because she was the mother of all living.* Archangel Jophiel casts them from the garden, and from the garden they go. *I will greatly multiply thy sorrow and thy conception; in sorrow thou shalt bring forth children.* Jophiel, Jophiel, you have many names. To the souls in heaven you teach all the languages of the earth. Then retire to your corner of cloud and close your eyes. Listen to the language swelling up to the sky.

Exhibit: AL 288-1

Picture yourself in a boat on a river. Leaning over the edge to find your reflection. In the night, you wake not knowing who you are. Your face morphs and eddies. Swirls like a stranger. A girl with kaleidoscope eyes. But oh, you are marvelous. You are marvelous. You are—

Exhibit: AL 288-1

Jophiel, guardian of the books, pour over your index of names. Jophiel. Yefefiah. Iofel. Yofiel. Which is you? Which your reflection in the mirror?

Exhibit: AL 288-1

The exhibit holds the angel Jophiel. Holds the girl with kaleidoscope eyes. Holds Eve, mother of all living, and holds her mitochondria, coiled tight like a spring. The exhibit holds me and the exhibit holds you. The exhibit holds so much language it may soon burst open like a womb.

Exhibit: AL 288-1

Lucy cannot breathe. Not enough air in this glass box. Smashes her body up against its panes. Pounds her fists. Screams. Screams. She does not belong in here. There has been some mistake. The box feels so crowded and tight. God, somebody let her out. And she opens her mouth to say, *This is not me*, but instead what she says is, *Picture yourself on a train in a station.* Steps back from the glass and in its surface, sees a face not her own.

Exhibit: AL 288-1

Dinkinesh. You are marvelous. You are *mother of all living.* You are Lucy in the sky. You are the exhibit. You are not you.

Exhibit: AL 288-1

And whose is this face? If you stare at your reflection and see a face, can it be said that the face is not yours? Can it be said that the body you inhabit, the name to which you answer, the plaque above your box, the DNA coiling in your chromosomes—is not you?

The glass is fogged with fingerprints. Hers, she thinks. But maybe not. Museum-goers approach her display case, read the text on the wall, rap nails against the glass. She wants to ask them to let her out, or at least to tell her who or what she is. But she fears what she'll say if she speaks. And then Dina reappears. Sits in front of the case with a notebook in her lap, writing, and every so often tears out a page and tapes it to the wall. Lucy presses her face to the glass to read what Dina has written. But the angle is wrong. *Is this it?* she asks, and floods with relief when the words are what she meant them to be. *Is this the center? Is this the end? Don't be ridiculous,* says Dina. *Give me more credit than that.*

Nathan the evolutionary psychologist is up close to the display case, notebook in hand. He peers at Lucy, chews on his pencil. *Those things that are the oldest parts of us are also the truest parts of us,* he says. *We study our origins to learn what is fundamental.* Dina continues to write. *What is a label?* she asks. She has a pincushion instead of tape now, and is stabbing the papers into the ground like butterflies in a collection. *I keep getting them wrong. Am I even getting any closer?*

EXHIBIT: AL 288-1

1974. On the sloping wall of an Ethiopian gully, a fragment of humerus. A skull shard nearby, and also bits of femur, vertebrae, pelvis, ribs, jaw. A body scattered in the soil, whitish knobs and shards waiting to be fitted back together. The team sections off the site and sets up camp. What brought them here was a hunch, the team leader will later claim. Something in the stomach, a bodily knowledge. And these are scientists, so they will not publicly make much of such coincidences, but in their hearts they will wonder. The first night at the camp, they celebrate with steak, mashed potatoes, cans of malt beer. Somewhere, a Beatles album plays on a loop. The men have dirt in their socks, dirt under their nails. *Cellophane flowers of yellow and green / towering over your head.* This place indeed feels otherworldly to them. An ancient place. One man thinks about the absurdity of this thing called time, the way they hold in their possession bones of a creature some three million years old and in the company of these bones play music featuring electric guitar and tambura. *Lucy in the sky with diamonds / Lucy in the sky with diamonds / Lucy in the sky.* And he says, *Hey. Hey, let's name her Lucy.* A hunch brought them to this place. A trick of acid and ash preserved these bones. So to name her after the song that happened to be playing, from a tape someone happened to toss in their bag as they packed—feels apt. *Let's name her Lucy.* And the men nod and cheer his suggestion and raise their aluminum cans in a toast—*To Lucy!* And the man who suggested the name grins and drinks. But after a while he slinks off to his tent, where he draws the flap closed and he weeps. Weeps. All of life and death, such random affairs. Every narrative we tell ourselves, such a pack of lies. The men, all day, wondering about the life this hominin lived. But it is all speculation. It is all fiction, even this present moment, even the thoughts he thinks as he stands here in the dark of his tent. The thin canvas doing little to conceal the revelry of the men beyond. What are they doing here, in this part of the world that is actually no older than any other? What are they doing digging in the dirt? The story they'll tell when they get back will construct a starting point that makes this end seem fated. But it isn't. He puts his face in his hands. Everything could so easily be other than it is.

Nathan finishes reading. Folds his arms and frowns. *What?* says Dina. *What's wrong with it? What does it say?* pleads Lucy, face against the glass again. *It's just,* says Nathan. *Just what? It's just that there is a difference. Between fact and fiction. Between science and lies. Some things are true. Some things we know to be true.* In the glass case, Lucy tries to enumerate the things she knows to be true. Nathan says, *You do science a disservice. You discredit the institution. What are the things you know to be true,* Lucy is desperate to say, but instead she says, *Language is a behavior that does not fossilize.* Nathan's frown deepens. *I'm going now,* he says. *Lacking orangutans, I'd like to observe the mating practices of the gorillas.* He turns and leaves. Dina approaches the glass case. *I'm sorry for leaving you. And I'm sorry for keeping you in here. I just hoped to contain you for a moment. Long enough to figure you out.* A breeze blows and Dina's many papers flutter like white wings. *AL 288-1* flashes: there, there, there. Dina unlocks the display case.

Adoption papers coat the table. She sees her name written out for the first time in months, not just once, but dozens of times. Leaping up at her in clean ink. A strange shape. Lucy. Lucy. LUCY. The letters increasingly unfamiliar. A name whose origins she does not know. Who gave it to her—a nurse? Social worker? First foster parents? Why did they choose it? What does it mean? No one has given her any mythology to go along with this name, so in her head, she keeps a list of other Lucys. I Love Lucy. Lucy from Peanuts. Lucy, the youngest of the Pevensey children. And then her most recent Lucy—the old, old skeleton her sixth grade teacher told her about. A missing link, he said, between apes and humans. *They called her Lucy after the Beatles song. Do you know the Beatles song?* She didn't, but she went home and listened to it over and over until she settled into a strange and misty space. She liked how unreal she felt, listening to that song. She liked that there were enough Lucys for her to choose from. What happens when two things share the same name? What is a name that does not point? These are not questions that concern her. Her name is porous; she clings to it anyway.

Autumn in Naperville. The leaves beginning to change, reds and yellows running like watercolors. The first crisp brown ones skating in the gutter. Lucy stands outside the Naperville museum, staring at the old familiar buildings, the outhouse, the chapel. She has not gone in since Dani's death. She misses it, this place thick with objects and stories. The rest of town seems bland and blank in comparison. But she is too afraid to go back in. Afraid she has begun to believe in ghosts.

She turns and heads again for home. Searches the path for dying worms to kill. Finds none.

When she enters her bedroom, her dresser drawers are all open. Empty hangers in the closet. Her foster mom, who is stuffing a duffel bag full of clothes, looks up. *Good, you're home. Hurry, go grab your toothbrush. You're almost packed. Where am I going?* asks Lucy. But her foster mom just says, *Is Dani with you? Make sure she's with you.*

Fifteen minutes later they are packed into the family sedan with several pieces of luggage and are turning onto the interstate. *Where are we going?* Lucy tries again. *Our petition got denied. They were going to take you.* Lucy sits stiffly and stares straight out the windshield. *Don't worry, Dani honey. I promise everything will be fine.*

They drive for a long time without stopping. The road rapidly loses its familiarity. She sees signs bearing town names she does not know. When she needs to pee, her foster mom hands her a water bottle with a wide opening. Around dinnertime, she passes her a tin of Altoids.

Sometime after midnight, they pull into a little motel with half its neon letters out. There are bugs in the sink and Lucy counts their corpses. She and her foster mom sleep in the same bed, though Lucy cannot sleep. She lies awake and looks out the gap between the curtains. The parking lot dark and still, occasional car on the street beyond. Her foster mom, asleep, has reached out a hand and placed it on Lucy's shoulder. Just holding it there. Then, around four a.m., a police car pulls into the lot. Lucy watches impassively as it parks, headlights going dark. The doors open and two officers step out. Boots on asphalt. A rapping at the door.

She stands at Poughkeepsie Station until her hair is saturated with rain. Then she buys a ticket and climbs on board. The train feels smoother than it should. As if the tracks are frictionless. As if this is a dream, and she is not on the earth but floating above it. She tries to picture herself as a toddler on this train. Recalls the details from the police report. Tries, as she has many times, to invent some story to account for ending up there. Then she is thinking of the *National Geographic* cover in the hospital lobby: *She's Here: Lucy Tours the U.S.* The eeriness of it. Lucy the Australopithecus has long been her favorite of the Lucys. After the police knocked on their motel room door, after they pulled her from her screaming foster mother's arms, after they sent her to a group home, and then another foster family, and another, she found herself at a city library. The book in her hands contained two pictures of Lucy: on the one hand, the bones. Shards mostly. Splinters. Teenage Lucy could identify the ribs, pelvis, and jaw, but the others remained cryptic. She might not have guessed they were bones at all, if not for the caption. And on the next page, across from the skeletal remains, an artistic reconstruction of what Lucy might have looked like while alive. Small soft body. Bright keen eyes. Such human hands. From a mere forty percent of the skeleton, a whole life imagined. The gaps filled, the fragments reassembled. Beneath the image, the caption: *Lucy, also known as Dinkinesh (Amharic word meaning "You are marvelous"), may very well be an early mother to us all.* You are marvelous. You are marvelous.

Yes. And so three years later, when starting college, Lucy declared a major in anthropology.

A woman sits opposite her on the train. They make eye contact and exchange smiles. *Where are you heading to, dear?* asks the woman. *I'm not sure,* replies Lucy. The woman smiles again. *And what's your name?* Lucy pauses. *Dinkinesh,* she says. *But you can call me Dina for short.*

Dina and Lucy, standing face to face. Standing face to face, Lucy and Dina. I know. I know you know. I know you know I know. *I am a thing of your mind,* says Dina. Dani. Dina. Dani. *You know it. I know you know it. Yes,* says Lucy. *I know. After all, you always understood the things that I said. Remember what you were told,* says Dina. *The origin of language was always the origin of misunderstanding. So what now?* asks Lucy. *We were looking for the center, weren't we?* says Dina. OH 7 still clinking in the air. Lucy nods. Onward they go.

They pass a herd of antelope. Springbok, pure white, leaping in the air with backs arched, legs stiff, heads pointing down. The honest signals of youth. A fitness telling predators: do not bother, you will not win. White body pulled like a puppet up, up, up, muscles contracting, curling, clenching, up, up, up, a milky white rhythm in all the cool and gentle green. The arc of this animal cannot lie. It plays like a reel: up, up, up, bright crescent in the green grass. Flex and leap programmed into it, its body beating out a code unlike any language. Could she learn to communicate this way? Whole body naming itself? An alphabet born from the shapes of muscles. There would be no gap then, between the signal and the thing signaled. They would be one and the same, and they would be nothing but true.

But then she thinks of what she would lose: story and memory and myth. All things imagined and alternative. There would be no speaking, then, of things not right at hand. *That which we cannot reach we still can speak of.* But not this animal. It can only signal itself. It can only spring up, up, up in this bright proof.

We're here, says Dina. *We're here.*

Lucy looks around. The sun spins white directly overhead. The horizon feels very far. Before her, there are strange marks in the ground, a series of oblong indentations arranged in lines. *This is it?* she asks. *This is the center?* She steps forward, crouches down. Very lightly touches the earth. The impressions are longer than they are wide, and the rock that holds them is the color of mud but hardened with age. *What am I looking at?* asks Lucy. *You know,* says Dina. *I know you know.* She points. Nearby is a plaque bearing text. Lucy stands. The plaque is the largest she's seen yet, spilling off its podium and stretching along the ground like a waterfall feeding a river. It's so long it disappears into the nearby brush, snaking away through the dropseed and finger grass. She steps closer. Looks down and begins to read.

EXHIBIT: LAETOLI FOOTPRINTS

So here we are: you, reading this text, and me, writing it. At the beginning. The beginning aches to unravel, like a skein frenzied to thread. I have ceased to believe in beginnings. And yet, here I am, beginning. What else to do?

And so: let us begin.

1983. In a flat in a Nairobi suburb, Mary Leakey, age seventy, pulls her tea bag in and out of her tea. Takes a sip. Puts it down. Begins: *How on earth does one get talked into these things? Publishers will talk one into anything.* An afternoon storm brews outside and the typewriter punches holes in the silence. *This is the first paragraph and I'm already regretting it.* She keeps the flat dark to rest her aging eyes; there is only the lamp on her desk and the greyish light from the window, falling like a pale tombstone across the carpet. *I'm sure that an autobiography, like any other book, needs a structure to hold it together. Archaeologists often divide things into three stages, usually "lower," "middle," and "upper" if they are thinking stratigraphically.* She pauses, fingers still on the keys, to watch a kingfisher alight on a wire outside. Her dalmatian sleeps with his big warm head on her feet. Three dogs dead in the past year. She buried them in the cold dirt of the yard and left their graves unmarked. If she focuses, she can feel the slight lift and fall of the dog's breath. She fears he will wake as the thunder nears. Tea steam curls. She watches it unthread, thin, disappear. The silence, if listened to hard, reveals itself to hold much sound. That distant ubiquitous rush, traffic or a somewhere storm. Also the breath of the dog. Lift and fall. *Afterwards, of course, they argue that the whole thing was continuous anyhow and that the divisions are arbitrary and for convenience only.* The rain sweeps down. The kingfisher flees.

1896. The boat, docked at Mombasa after fourteen days at sea. The men streaming off the gangplank into the sticky humidity. The air has a different weight from Karachi, where they boarded, a city so dry the men doubted it was coastal at all. Then the Arabian coming into view, big silver impossibility. Now the water won't leave them alone, hangs invisible in the air, glues their hair and clothes and skin together. Tomorrow they will be sweating in this heat, carrying beams of eucalyptus and steel, spiking the first of over a million railway ties into the earth. The men, who speak nothing but Punjabi, quizzed each other in English on the boat. *Good morning. Good evening. Good night.* Over thirty thousand of them will arrive in the months to come, recruited from the poorest villages in the Punjab. They come carrying contracts for three years of labor at twelve rupees a month. Twenty-five hundred of them will not survive these three years. Their remains will be cremated in the camps, but their smoke will be nothing like the smoke of the train, those thick oily coils. The men roll their heads around on their necks. Listen to the click and grind of bone. Foreign phrases sound in their minds, repeatedly, in voices unlike their own: *Good morning. Good evening. Good night.*

1925. A memory: strange dance of lamplight on rock. Limestone, calcite, flicker, shadow. She stands in the cave and stares up at its wall. A painted bestiary—red, black, brown. There are horses and bison, mammoth and ibex, rhinos, reindeer, cattle, wolves. The animals' bodies conform to the contours of rock—the bison's spine spans a convexity, the ibex kneels on the floor of the cave. *Charcoal and clay, ground to powders,* says a voice behind her. *Mixed with water, animal fat, blood.* Another voice says, *Incredible. Isn't it, Mary?* The voice is her father's. Mary tries to conceive of the length of fifteen thousand years. Cannot. Has no scale with which to gauge such a span of time. *Who were they?* she asks. *Cro-Magnon man,* replies the first voice. *Of the Upper Paleolithic.* Words that mean nothing to her. Earlier, they hunted scraps of flint along the river. Mary cupped the dirt in her hands, then let it slowly drain; the feeling was one of sucking, of emptiness turning solid. *Ah ha!* She looked up; her father held between his thumb and finger a slender flint blade. *Imagine, Mary. Imagine all the earth this full.* So now she puts her hand to the cold rock of the cave. The old pigment. Accretions of centuries, mineral rough and worn. Hoof and pelt blurred beneath. *Who were they?* She is unable to feel what she wants to feel. Digs her hand harder into the rock. Presses and grinds until she feels the break of skin. Sharp sting. When she examines her hand, there is her own bright blood, riddled with grit.

1983. Mary knows about superposition and I know what Mary knows. Or rather: I know about superposition and Mary knows what I know. Or rather: we both know about superposition but not about each other. Or rather. Or rather. I know what Mary knows because Mary does not exist. Mary knows what I know because Mary exists inside of me. I know what Mary knows because I have imagined it, and knowledge is only imagination to begin with.

Mary knows about superposition. Superposition: how the earth wears its time in stripes. This, the first law of stratigraphy—the oldest layers are at the bottom. You must begin at the end, dig back to the beginning. Time is never chronological, and the beginning is always farther back than you believe.

Time is never chronological? No. It comes to us in slips and scraps. Chronology is the shape we arrange.

And Mary arranges. Stratigraphically. The oldest layers first: her birth, her parents, her childhood. But much is missing. Unconformity: a gap in geologic time. The rock, and so the record, has been worn away. Some things cannot be reclaimed. *Like everyone else I find it almost impossible to distinguish between what really are direct early memories of my own and the stories of my childhood that others have repeated.... Perhaps it doesn't matter very much.*

She looks up. The window. Sky pale, bright, blank. Something like aluminum. She will not trace the shape of forgetting again.

1896. *Crosstie crosstie crosstie crosstie. Gauge. Gauge. Spike spike spike spike.* It's the sledgehammer overhead, it's the driving of the metal into the hard crust of earth that drains you fastest. It's the ache of muscles and the grind of shoulder bone in socket. *Spike spike spike spike.* The noise. A million small collisions, metal on metal, like a violent clang of bells. *Crosstie crosstie crosstie crosstie. Gauge. Gauge. Spike spike spike spike.* The sun on the steel is both bright and dull. The second it takes for the sledgehammer to complete its downward arc feels like some slow eternity. Time balloons as the hammer falls, expanding to let the minds of the men remember they are minds. The work is otherwise numbing, otherwise forbids memory, turns their bodies to nothing but body. But in the endlessness of the hammer's fall there is room for so much thought. Room to doubt the possibility of another single swing, room to mourn the softness of rivers and wheat back home, room to feel half mad with longing and loneliness and deep, deep fatigue. And then hammer hits nail and they are jarred from themselves once again.

1926. Curtains drawn. A sour smell, pail of vomit by the bed. Needle sliding in her father's skinny arm. Slow plunge of morphine. A bead of blood. He coughs, a scraping, hacking cough, bringing with it reddish sputum. Standing in the doorway, Mary knows he will die.

In the globe of her grief she takes many long walks. Crisscrosses the *causse,* the limestone plateau her father told her once formed the bed of a great ocean. How, she still wonders, could an ocean floor be lifted up like a mountain? How could trilobite and nautilus, creatures of the sea, appear encased in rock at these great heights? He explained it to her, about plates of earth crashing together, but she has trouble believing it. She sits on the forest floor, looks around, tries to imagine this place submerged. Bluish bubbles, their upward wobble. It is spring, and the trees are beginning to green. Sealed crocuses poke from the soil, and there is a mushroom, huge and airy as a loaf of bread. A rustle in the bushes. She looks up to see a pair of red foxes tumbling in play, nipping at each other's necks and butting heads. She sits very still. Tries to watch the foxes without thinking a single thing. To observe and nothing else. But in spite of herself, she wonders where this rock will be a hundred million years from now. Wonders if these foxes' bones, and her father's, and her own, will rest underwater, will drift, homeless, in a world not their own.

1928. In the backseat of her uncle's Model T, Mary watches the flashing Wiltshire farmland. She's been silent the whole car ride, nearly three hours, despite her mother and uncle's occasional attempts to engage her in conversation. This is only partly out of contempt, and partly out of her total absorption in the countryside, its wind and green and smell of manure.

The thin white road takes a turn and her uncle stops the car. Before them, Stonehenge rises grey against a grey sky. Like bad teeth, Mary thinks. She exits the car. Approaches. The height of the stones shocks her. They are magnificent, in their size, in their improbability. If a scrap of chipped flint suggests to her a life as full and dear as her own, what do these monoliths suggest? Almost too much to imagine. But as magnificent as they are, they are at the same time pitiful. Ramshackle, in pieces, as if they've just been dropped. Like a child's scattered blocks after her tower has collapsed. How much labor, how many men and how many years, to get these stones from one place of the earth to another, to stack and arrange them in this ring? And for what? *It's a burial ground,* says her uncle. *See? Barrow mounds all around.* He points. The grassy slopes appear to look inward toward the rocks. As if something momentous is happening in the center of the circle. But there is nothing in the center of the circle. There is nothing here but stone and corpse. Mary drops to a low boulder. The grey of rock and sky blurs into a single cold wash. The wind pulls tears from her eyes.

1986. Mary's outline: *parents, grandparents—Freres, John, Doug, Cecilia—genetics—archeological interest inherited?—parents meet in Egypt—Great War—Lincoln St.—doll at Christmas from Molly, Marty, Toudy—father's painting—Italy—legs pulled off live frogs—cyclamen, cherries—the peeling green paint—*

1928. The peeling green paint on her windowsill, which she scrapes at slowly. Pigment gritting up under her nail, the rough wood revealing itself beneath. She scrapes and scrapes to expose what has been hidden until a splinter breaks off in her skin.

1986. The kettle shrieking. Mary at her typewriter, not typing, not rising, letting the shriek build to a sharp pitch. *Perhaps it doesn't matter very much.* Stares at the sentence. Considers. Around her, the air splits with steam and sound. The moment slows, expands, sags. What amount of shrieking before evaporation is complete? *Perhaps it doesn't matter very much.* Will she allow such a sentence to stand? Does she believe it at all? She sits and stares and the kettle shrieks and shrieks.

1895. Five thousand miles away, in a turreted palace of limestone and iron, 1,400 men in top hats and tails debate the fate of the East Africa Protectorate. They are balding and bespectacled, sport thick white beards and occasionally wigs. One man stands and declares that *four if not five powers are steadily advancing towards the upper waters of the Nile. If this house continues to hesitate with the construction of a railway, we will lose Uganda—and after that the Suez Canal, and after that India!* This is language that has lasted. That has survived intact. The words ring darkly under the vaulted ceiling. The words persist throughout the decades. In 1895 the men shift in their seats. There is urgency and fear in them, and also delight. A railway—clean, bright, all steam and steel. Powerful and huge. Some few resist, citing the cost, but there is no stopping them now. *We have taken over this country for better or worse,* declares the man on his feet. *For better,* the others think. *Surely for better.* The vote passes. The railway begins.

It is tempting to think of it as they did: a linear journey, beginning at Mombasa, overcoming many obstacles, ending triumphantly on the shores of Lake Victoria. Easy to think of each hammer fall as the sound of progress, the indomitable human spirit, defiance of all odds. Beginning, middle, end. To avoid such thinking, let's get the end out of the way now. The end is a white woman in a long white dress, driving home the final key. She is the foreman's wife—has been there on the sidelines these five years, keeping herself carefully contained in a pool of parasol shade. She places her parasol on the ground now and, for the first time, picks up a tool. Five white men are there also, and they chortle good-naturedly at her clumsy sledgehammer swing. The lake brightly laps. Afterward, in England, *The Times* prints a massive Union Jack on its front page and declares, *This great and arduous undertaking has been brought to a successful conclusion.* It condemns the naysayers, who *were loath to recognize the responsibilities which a great imperial possession involves.* In the halls of Buckingham Palace, the railroad's chief engineer will kneel and be knighted by a queen wielding a sword. *The Times* declares that *The Pax Britannica has secured order and security over a vast region of nearly 4,000,000 souls which until the advent of British rule was given over to a cruel and sterilizing tyranny.* The white men chortle but think simultaneously that she is a lovely sight, all dressed in white, lace bright against the blue lake light. And the foreman's wife giggles, straightening and handing the hammer to her husband. He kisses her cheek and says, *Well done, my dear,* then takes another few swings just to be safe. This is the end, here, now, as the first train reaches the rail's terminus, clanking wearily from its long and arduous journey. This is arrival, this is completion, this the place the champagne is popped and the flutes raised foaming with cries of *To England!* This is the destination to which everything has been hurtling, pistons pumping like mad, corpses and coal going up in smoke. This is progress, this is destiny, this is the civilizing arc of time. This is the story's end—for those who believe in such things.

•

1896. The boat, docked at Mombasa after fourteen days at sea. The port has the feeling of being overrun, unable to absorb the shiploads of equipment and men it is continually asked to. There is debris upon the beach. There are many slanted masts in the air, haphazard as kindling. Crates and crates of rivets. Men streaming off the gangplank. With them, a boy of seventeen who will tell nobody his name. He has not said a word the entire trip, has moved so soundlessly through the ship the other men call him *bhūta*—ghost. And as he steps for the first time from the British ship onto the African soil, he thinks: there could be no better name.

1933. St. John's College rises above her, the main gate crenelated as if for battle. Such a barrage of symbols: flowers and crosses and crowns, an eagle, a chalice, a half dozen fleurs-de-lis. A pair of strange beasts, perhaps some species of antelope, filigreed with gold. Though only four hundred years old, it is as cryptic to her as any relic of prehistory. She enters. Follows the directions she's been given and, upon arriving at her destination, knocks on the door.

He welcomes her. Points her to a crate on the desk. Inside, a grid of partitions, and in each square, a stone hand ax. *You've been excavating at Hembury the past few summers, isn't that right?* But she is already focused on the glassy black obsidian, so different from the flint she's used to. Already she's thinking about the challenge of representing such stone—how it shears away in curves and coils. She can see in it the shapes of waves, a memory of liquid. *Igneous.* A stone to make you believe in change, in loss, in a thing made forever other than it is. So unlike sedimentary rock, in which particles are preserved for eons. The dust of time, broken down and further down but never destroyed. But this obsidian is sleek and clean. Old as it is, you would not know it.

Dr. Leakey loads the box into her arms. She promises him the illustrations within the month. *Many thanks. I think they'll really bring the book to life, you know? My pleasure, Dr. Leakey,* says Mary. *Please,* he says. *Please call me Louis.*

Only a matter of time, then, before his fingers are at the buttons of her shirt, before her hands are twining in his hair. In the evenings he teaches her cat's cradle—loops both their hands with string and shows her slowly how to slip fingers in and out. A mere three miles away, his pregnant wife tucks their two-year-old daughter into bed. *Little fingers move over pointer finger nooses and pick up the far thumb strings. Release thumbs.* Just outside the window, the Bridge of Sighs arcs over the river. Light soft on greenish water. He guides her fingers. His, rough and large. *Thumbs move under the pointer finger nooses. Pick up the near and far strings from the little fingers. Release the little fingers.* The strings shift their tension from here to there, taut then slack then taut. He tells her about growing up in Kenya, where he built his own hut at age eleven, adding a second and then a third house by the time he was fourteen. *When I entered Weymouth at seventeen I was bewildered. Really, I'm more a Kikuyu than an Englishman.* His fingers slide the string with ease. *Pointer fingers come up through the center of the triangle.* Our dexterous fingers. When our hands evolved, so did the rest of us. Tool-making demands complex, hierarchical, sequential thought patterns—neural networks that may have been coopted by the brain's communication center. Grammar and syntax, not so unlike the formation of stone tools. *Middle fingers move over and through the pointer finger nooses; pull both far thumb strings through.* Could sequence be so much. This then this then this then this. First he unbuttons her blouse. Then puts his mouth on her throat. She feels something building in her. Something climbing. Their clothes heaped on the floor. Light from the window settling in the folds: cotton and shadow and setting sun. His fingers on her nipples now. Blood rushes to various parts of their bodies. Heart rates speed. They are gasping and panting. They are on the bed and their fingers are clawing at shoulders and backs. What is this drive toward climax? The rising tension, like an arrow to a target. Bodies satisfying a desire they themselves have created. Buildup and release, swelling and sighing. These ancient and aching rhythms. He finishes with a shudder and a groan. She drops a loop of string and the whole thing falls loose.

1933. His wife's baby is born in December. He sits in the hospital waiting room while she sweats and pants in tangled sheets. Her skin tears somewhat when the child comes.

After the birth, he finally tells her: there is another woman—he is leaving. Leaving her, with the toddler and the infant, with her breasts full of milk and her stomach still loose and hanging. And his wife, an archeologist herself, thinks: are we really just our biologies? She'd always considered the story of human origins to be a series of disruptions. This work, a search for the moment—some great rupture—when humans became humans. But now she thinks, it is more like a series of continuities. It is the study of how humans were never more than animals to begin with.

1934. *Dear Mary. Before leaving Kanam two years ago, I placed into the earth several iron markers, identifying the site where my skull was found. Upon returning, I am greatly dismayed to discover the markers missing. Pulled up, no doubt, by local fishermen, who use the metal for their spears and harpoons. While you know I am sympathetic to the plight of the Kenyan natives, whom I consider practically my own kin, I* *confess myself cross. These people have no conception of what surrounds them, the wealth of knowledge that lies in wait beneath their feet. It pains me to think of what might have been lost, merely for a little catch of catfish! Of course, we took photographs of the site, but as luck would have it, they came out blank. Furthermore, the rains have been such that the land has changed beyond my recognition. I have no hope of orientation. This is most unlucky timing, as Mr. Boswell arrives any day. An endorsement from him would do much to persuade those who doubt the age of the Kanam skull. But Boswell himself is still skeptical, and tends to place his hopes for early* Homo *in that amateur Dawson and his Piltdown Man. So be it. I am convinced, whatever my colleagues may wish to believe, that early man originated here, in the wilds of East Africa, and not in a hamlet in East Sussex.*

I eagerly anticipate your arrival and look forward to the help you will offer me once we are at Olduvai, which simply begs for further excavation. I hope you can tolerate it, though—it is nothing but dust, dust, dust!

Give my best to your mother, if she'll let you. Much love. Louis.

1935. Cape Town harbor glitters bluegreen. January sun pours over the water, painting it with reflected sails and hulls. Mary and her mother stand on the deck as the liner moves, ponderous and heavy, into dock. The horizon is broken by the huge plateau of Table Mountain, its flat surface lifting like an altar. Along the coast, waves hurl themselves at the cliffs, exploding white with spray. The single word in Mary's mind is: *Africa.*

Mary's mother has brought her on this trip hoping it will cause her to forget Louis. But Louis is all she can think of. Louis and Africa are, to her, bound up in each other. *I'm more a Kikuyu than an*

Englishman. And she fell in love with him for this. He is as out of place in England as she is. And so now, as she stares up at the stunning white rush of Victoria Falls, she is thinking of him. The water falls as if outside of time. Pouring over the cliff's edge, the river's calm glass splits into wild ropes of white. Collides with rock at the bottom and erupts in rainbow haze. She feels herself positioned as if on a lip of cliff like this; ready to pour over and plunge.

1986. Mary's kettle screaming and she staying very still. Kitchen roiling with steam. *Perhaps it doesn't matter very much.* Droplets gathering on the panes of the window. Collecting and then falling out of themselves.

1896. The men live in tents that flood during rain or in metal sheds thick with ticks and fleas. A full fifty percent of them are sick with malaria. The makeshift hospitals overcrowded, patients lie on soaked grass floors, gripped with fever and with chills, sweating and vomiting and shaking and shitting. There are no proper doctors, only field medics with little training, who measure heart rates and drag dead bodies from the beds. The new occupants are then lifted into the soiled sheets to spend their final hours in a bed that stinks of a stranger's shit. And outside, still, the thwack of steel on steel. Still, the rail's slow and biting creep.

1935. Mary's mother, having failed at her task, departs in tears to take a boat back to England, while Mary boards a plane headed for Louis and Tanzania. She feels wild and bold, crossing the African continent alone. Looks out the window at the verdant green, the darkblue gash of Lake Malawi, feels giddy to be above all this, to have this vast expanse contained for once in a single tableau. *A f r i c a.*

Louis is late to pick her up. She waits and waits at the airport, but it's the rainy season and many roads are run to mud. She sits in the airport's little lobby with a cup of tea, listening to the distant-engine sound of thunder. The British couple across from her advises her not to worry. *You'll soon learn how it is,* the woman says. *No journey runs on schedule here. This is a wild country.* They suggest she get a hotel; her beau will no doubt be here in the morning.

And when morning arrives, Mary rises and goes to her window. The curtain of cloud has parted—Kilimanjaro reveals itself, huge and snow-capped and stunning. Could it really have been so thoroughly concealed by cloud? And can it really rise so wintry and blue above this tropical and forested land? She thinks of all she has already seen: the Atlantic shores of Cape Town, somehow so much brighter and bluer than the same ocean back home. Victoria Falls turning and twisting, like a beast in heat. The low scrubby plants of the desert, jeweled with yellow blooms, as if bragging of a beauty stronger than the dryness and scorch. *This is a wild country.* And when Louis does finally arrive, she takes him to her hotel room and they fuck pressed up against the window. Behind her, Kilimanjaro crowning again with cloud, and beyond, the Serengeti, where Louis will take her soon, where they will plumb the earth for bones, where, together, they will expose the secrets of this wild and ancient land.

1896. Coco palms felled by the hundreds. Thwack of blade on trunk—the long slow sweep—then fatal final crash. Timber sliced into planks and boards. Machinery on the beach, all hiss and clank and thud, blackening the sand, smearing the water with oil and ash.

The horizon loses itself in haze; the sun is a cigarette tip in the sky. Advance parties penetrate the interior, clearing swaths for the rail. The country is an enemy. Baobabs thick as watchtowers, thorn trees spiked like an arsenal, all linked by a chainmail of creeping vine. They slice and thwack. Slice and thwack. Above them, homeless birds circle and cry. Behind, a growing wound gapes its mouth. This was never anything but battle.

1935. Ngorongoro crater opens before them like a gasp. The caldera bluing with morning mist. A vast, lush carpet of grass and rain, broken by occasional outcroppings of rock and cloud-like acacias. The sky is dappled—here, rainclouds, bruise-dark; there, golden sun, pouring like a balm. *Caldera,* she whispers to herself. It sounds like *cradle.*

They cross the plains. In time, Olduvai Gorge comes into view—a dark scar, softened by distance and the haze of heat. The earth opening wide, as if longing to yield up its dead.

When they reach the camp, Louis introduces her to his lead fossil hunter, a Kikuyu man named Heslon Mukiri. Mary, in her Nairobi apartment in 1986, will describe him and Louis as *lifelong friends and virtually scientific colleagues.* She will write that he was skeptical of her, a woman, the only woman working at the Gorge. That she had to work to earn his respect. I imagine Mary dressing each morning in her tent. Khakis and a collared shirt. Brushing her hair. Aiming for pretty but not too pretty. Aiming for qualified, assured, and just masculine enough. Feeling instead tall and lanky and awkward. In 1986, Mary will write that her reason for doing the work she did was simple curiosity. Louis thinks knowledge of the past will help people to understand and control the future. But not Mary. She believes human activity will follow its irreversible patterns. What will happen will happen and it is out of her hands. But the past is different. The past must be sought out, pieced back together, deliberately, intentionally. The future will exist without her, but the past depends on her to bring it into being. People forget that the definition of *history* is not *the past*, but rather, *the written record of the past.* Rather, *the past as it exists on paper.*

There is no paper which bears Heslon Mukiri's reasons for doing the work he does. Perhaps he believes, as Mary does, that the past cannot exist without him. Or perhaps he believes the opposite: that the past will be created whether he participates or not. That too many things have been taken from him, and he would like to get some of them back. I imagine Mary imagining Heslon. Searching his face for the skepticism she is convinced he harbors. Watching his figure retreat across the Gorge and envying what she perceives he has: a sense of belonging, of ownership, of a right to be here and to preside over this place. She grips a chisel in her fist and for the briefest flash of a second imagines bringing it down on Heslon Mukiri's skull. Then is startled by such a thought. Disturbed. So unsettling, the way certain impulses simply intrude, unbidden, uncharacteristic. She is not a violent person. Struggles even to eat the animals Louis hunts for dinner, and only does so to avoid appearing womanly and soft. No, she is not a violent person. Is free of such archaic and animal urges.

1896. Sunrise. The light fingers its way through the canvas to prod them in the eyes. They blink and groan. Drag themselves from bed. No water to wash. For breakfast, a little toast and tea. The supply train waits for them, steel bright in the mounting sun. They clamber aboard like shipwrecked men, lodging their bodies where they can. There is a jolt and the train begins to move.

The one they call ghost sits atop a crate of fishplates. The metal growing hot against his skin. His real name is Sukhjinder Saleem, and he recites this name over and over in his head, lest he forget it. But he does not want to say it out loud. He doesn't know why. Only it seems like giving something away. The contract he signed in Kirachi bears his name twice. Once, in his own hand, the familiar letters: ਸੁਖਜਿੰਦਰ ਸਲੀਮ. And once in the alien shape of the Latin alphabet: *Sukhjinder Saleem.* The first time he'd seen his name rendered as such. The first time he felt so wholly outside himself. No matter how long he stares at the Latin letters, they refuse to feel his own. How can that be me, he wonders. And he concludes that it is not him. It is instead a code, and those who can crack it can claim him as theirs. It is less like a name and more like a brand.

Also like a brand are these fishplates below him. The steel burns even through his clothing. Under his turban the sweat collects. For a moment, his mind becomes blank, emptied of language. He remembers nothing. There is heat and coal-stink and the terrible noise of the train. There are men speaking around him but he cannot hear their voices. The name of this place slips from him. All names, suddenly so very far.

1935. Lying on her side, brushing dirt from a bone. It is slow and careful work. Minute scraping of a dental pick, the delicate tap of a chisel. Watching the fossil reveal itself. Watching it take shape as the soil falls away. Shedding centuries like skin. They are excavating what appears to be a small herd of extinct antelope. *Phenocotragus recki.* She wonders what caused the death of the whole herd at once. Possibly some disease that struck hard and fast, took them all together. Or, more likely, predators—a pride of lions, a pack of hyenas. Perhaps even a tribe of early humans. She lets herself imagine it—their crouched and hairy forms, loping limbs and smallish skulls. But with eyes like hers—sparking and aware. Imagines them closing in around the kill. Frayed strings of muscle and fat, cage of rib poking from the meat. Imagines the humans advancing, slow but hungry, so very hungry, imagines them reaching for the prize, all at once, mouths dripping and pupils huge, imagines—

She jumps. Someone has just thumped her on the back. She spins around. But there is no one there.

1932. In the darkroom. Prints submerged in a chemical bath: silver halide and citric acid. The developer waits for the image to appear. Hills and the low scrubby bush, iron markers driven like spears. But they do not appear. There is only a blinding wash of light, overexposed and ghostly, like sun on chrome.

1935. *Did you move? Did you? Did anybody move? No, Mrs. Leakey. Nobody was anywhere near you.* Mary stares at the empty space where she felt the slap. The nearest workman was fifty feet off. And yet she felt it. She is sure. *Take a break,* says Louis when she goes to him. *Drink something. It's probably just the heat.* So she goes to her tent, sits on her mattress and sips from a canteen. Breathes. And after fifteen minutes she gets up, goes back to the antelope skeleton still half hidden in the earth, where she chides her spooked assistants as she might a child. *Stop this silliness,* she says when they hesitate to continue digging. *It was just the heat.* She stares at the skeleton, brownish and old. There is nothing sacred about it. Nothing magical. They are just old bones.

•

1896. The train arrives at railhead. The men climb down, scramble to unload the sleepers and rails so the train may reverse to camp for its next load. And then it's *crosstie crosstie crosstie crosstie. Gauge. Gauge. Spike spike spike spike.* Again and again, all day long, the sweat pouring from them in streams.

1936. The supply truck is late. For days they've eaten nothing but rice, sardines, apricot jam. Low on water, they drink from a stream in which rhinos have wallowed; the taste is of urine, no matter how long it's boiled. After a hard rain, they collect runoff from the tents, forgetting they've recently been sprayed with insecticide. Everybody falls ill. Not to mention, they are out of cigarettes. So Mary and Louis pack themselves into the lorry and head for the city.

The drive to Nairobi is long and slow on the rutted road. Dust billows. They bounce and jolt. At the border town of Pussumuru, they stop for a meal. The proprietor of an Indian market serves them rice, chicken, daal. *Any trouble on the road?* he asks in English. *None. Why?* asks Louis. *District Commissioner Grant. Murdered yesterday at Narok. By the Maasai.* There is worry in the man's voice. *Why?* asks Louis again. *Who knows?* says the man. *Some say he forced Maasai warriors to do road work. Others, that he stole their cattle to sell. Does it matter? The Maasai are a bloody people.* Mary and Louis exchange glances. *The commissioner can hardly have been blameless,* says Louis. The proprietor raises his eyebrows. *All I know is he's now face down in the dirt with a spear through his back. People here are frightened. We could not withstand a Maasai uprising. We're shopkeepers. Tradesmen.* The man's English is perfect.

They don't stay long at Pussumuru, but climb back into the lorry, hoping to make it to Nairobi before midnight. But an hour beyond the border, Louis takes a turn too fast and drives them off the road, into a deep gully. He revs and revs the engine, but the wheels are stuck. Night pools like a spill of ink. They have no choice; they curl up on blankets beside the car and sleep.

Morning finds them digging. Table knives and two enamel dinner plates as shovels. The sun steadily mounts and they begin to drip with sweat. A group of Maasai warriors gathers to watch, apparently amused. *Beneath their dignity to help, I suppose,* Mary huffs. But after the news at Pussumuru, neither she nor Louis wishes to provoke the men. So she keeps her head down and continues to dig. Feels a mounting frustration. How farcical it is. She feels a cartoon of herself, mucking around in the dirt like this. How childish she must appear in the eyes of the Maasai, who peer down at them from above. And, imperceptibly, embarrassment turns to rage. For a flash, she pictures their bodies skewered by spears. Then the image is gone. She is simply digging.

1935. There is much still to do at Olduvai, but other business draws them home. They board a ship at Mombasa, crates of fossils, stone tools, and soil samples in tow. The journey, through the Red Sea, the Suez Canal, and the Mediterranean, takes three weeks, during which Louis writes most of his new book on Kenya. Mary types it for him, on a portable typewriter in her cabin. He brings new pages each night. Mary types: *I was born and bred in Kenya, and I have spent the greater part of my life there.... In many ways I am more a Kikuyu than an Englishman.* She makes a mistake. Yanks the page out. Types it again. Louis is napping; the windowless rocking of their cabin affects him more than her. She types: *I want to make people in England realize that the greatest problem of all is that of winning the co-operation, friendship and trust of the natives and thus helping them to develop so that they can take their due place in the Empire.* She feels good about helping Louis, feels good about helping Kenya, feels nothing but good.

1896. They creep forward, managing about a half mile a day. But to the men, it doesn't feel like movement. Nothing about it feels like the word *forward*. At the end of each workday they take the train back to camp, then back to railhead the next morning, then back to camp, back to railhead, back to camp. They feel dizzied and spun. There is no map in their heads of where they are going, where they have been. The foreman, the chief engineer, the MPs ensconced at Westminster, they have the maps. They have the arrows pointing from here to there, from beginning to end. The men building the thing—for them, time hangs still as smoke. There is no arrow to it.

Every ten or fifteen miles, camp is shifted forward to the head of the line. The men pack their meager belongings. Pull tent pegs from the earth.

The new campsite is at the edge of a ravine. Four hundred feet wide, a deep green gash that brings them to a halt. For twenty-five days, not a single sleeper is laid. And time, which was simply solid and still, now turns liquid and twists.

1937. They spend a few years in a cottage in Hertfordshire, Louis writing his books, Mary typing them. The cottage has no electricity or heat, though it's unlikely they could afford to pay for either if they were available. They fetch water from a well, which must be warmed slowly on the kitchen range. There is an outhouse in the yard, its wood rain-warped and pale. In her free time, Mary plants dahlias and English roses, and for a moment forgets the other things that soil may hold. But only for a moment. While delivering a lecture at Oxford, Louis impresses his audience with his extensive knowledge of the customs, language, and tribal structure of the Kikuyu. Some months later, he receives an unexpected offer: funding for two years, salary and expenses, in order to undertake a comprehensive study of the tribe. And so the cottage is packed up, their Dalmatians sent to new homes, and Mary and Louis are on the boat for Mombasa once again. When they land, they make straight for Kiambaa and the home of Chief Koinange, a friend of Louis's and leader of the Kikuyu. *What if they say no?* asks Mary. *They won't say no,* says Louis. They wait in the chief's guesthouse while the council of elders debates Louis's request. It takes longer than either of them anticipated. They pace. Read a little. Try to imagine the conversation being held, imagine what objections might be being raised. But they cannot imagine. *They won't say no,* says Louis. And, in the end, they don't. Chief Koinange returns and grants Louis permission to write a book the chief himself will be unable to read. Louis thanks him, excited but unsurprised. To him, nothing makes more sense than that he should be allowed to tell this tale.

1896. The viaduct slowly spans the ravine, like the web of a giant spider. Timber trestles growing with the impression of a fractal, a shape repeating itself, replicating and unstoppable. When the ravine is finally bridged, the skies break with a rain so heavy they must wait another three weeks before any track can be laid. They sit in their threadbare tents and watch the mud floor flood, a floating leaf enter the tent like a ship. Time is a deluge. Too much of it. Is it just their imagination, or has the leaf circled back, has an actual current formed inside their tent, spiraling, spiraling, an unbroken loop?

•

Mary was no geologist, and nor am I, but we have both spent long hours studying stone. Attempting to decode stripes, crack the cipher of sediment, knowing rock as a thing to read. So many names for the rifts and faults and strata and plates, such a language to account for the history of mineral. This language cannot lie: it is what it says what it is. Or is it? The rock tells me about the rain, about the rivers, about the wind. But for everything it tells, there's another secret that it holds.

1939. After the grant runs out, the Leakeys are left without income. They take a very small house outside Nairobi so Louis may finish his book. When he does, it comes to a total of 700,000 words. His publisher balks at such a massive work. *Who on earth would purchase such a thing?*

And then Germany invades Poland. The news reaches them from such a distance it feels unreal. There is no question, now, of returning to England, not with war breaking out across Europe. They are safe where they are—the nearest enemy forces are the Italians in Ethiopia and Somalia, which may pose a threat to Kenya's northern border, but not to Nairobi or Tanzania to the south. The war is much like a myth to them, here in this land that has always felt set apart.

The war is real enough, however, to produce some badly needed employment for Louis. The British government enlists him to track down the sources of the anti-British propaganda that is proliferating across the country. His knowledge of Kenya and the Kikuyu make him an ideal choice, and they will pay him accordingly. As he carries out this work, he manages to supplement his pay by selling goods to the Kikuyu in remote villages, which he buys wholesale in Nairobi. Mostly, the demand is for patented medicines. Pills and syringes and vials. The rent gets paid; the war rages on.

Before long he's running guns. Brens, Brownings, Martini-Enfields, M1-Garands, supplied in abundance by the British authorities. He packs the lorry full, drives up to the border, unloads the weapons into the hands of Ethiopians who will not live long. Then he heads for home, but not before a quick detour to check out any local archeological sites, where he brushes dust from old dead bones and cradles them with care.

1940. The track must be dug up. Shifted several hundred meters west. Mary doesn't know or care precisely why. She only knows that, thanks to the vagaries of the railway authorities, soon the tracks will run straight through a known Neolithic site, rich with artifacts. They have given her three months. Three months to excavate the site before the rail destroys it for good. It is not enough time—in the single trench they have been permitted to dig, they have already found over 75,000 finished tools, and close to two million waste chips. How much more is still there, just feet below them, soon to be lost to the millennia?

To be honest, though, the artifacts are not all that interesting. Most are very similar—thousands of spear tips, virtually indistinguishable. There is no excitement, now, when she discovers one in the dirt. It is impossible to imagine all the lives that yielded these tools; impossible to give weight to that much mundanity. The cleavage of obsidian, its glassy ripples and curves, fascinated her once. Now, as she adds yet another specimen to her cardboard box, she feels slightly sickened. So many teeming creatures leaving their refuse on the earth. And here she is, dedicating her life to their preservation, gathering their trash as if into a reliquary. For what.

Mary is pregnant. She is trying to decide how amazed to be by this fact. Right now, her baby is a half inch of tissue, a tiny neural tube curling in on itself. She stares at a black rock flake in her palm and thinks of how unexceptional it all is. The most common thing in the world. She feels dumbfounded by scale: on the one hand, the tininess of a zygote. On the other, the unfathomable span of geologic time. Four and a half *billion* years. Her awe at the eons and her awe at her embryo have neutralized each other. She feels only depleted and tired.

Still, she continues to sort, dividing rocks into separate cardboard containers based on their ages. She is prepared for amazement to grip her again at any time—she will pluck yet another ordinary stone from the soil and, somehow, be struck by its reality, its age, its humanity. Sooner or later, it will happen. She continues to dig.

Later that year, after the new track has been laid and the train is chugging daily across it, termites will find their way into the cardboard boxes containing the not-yet-analyzed artifacts. When Mary next goes to the boxes, they will be gone, little more than a dust of pulp over the heaped obsidian. All 75,000 tools now inextricably mixed, run together like time turned liquid.

1940. The baby arrives. Louis is away, but this bothers Mary little. What use would he be in these early days anyway.

They give the baby both his grandfathers' names: Jonathan Harry Erskine Leakey. Mary likes having a baby about the same way she likes having a particularly good cup of tea. She thinks, with equanimity, that she is a success now, a far as natural selection is concerned. That, like a salmon or a spider, the best thing for her to do now would be to lie down and die. But of course, that wouldn't be a very good evolutionary strategy, human infants being far less self-sufficient than a salmon's fry or a spider's hatchlings. She stares at Jonathan Harry Erskine Leakey in his crib and thinks of how stupidly soft he is. And alongside her love, her urge to nurse and nourish, there is a tiny bloom of spite. He could not have been born all fleshy-skulled if nature did not know that she, Mary, would be there, could be relied upon to give everything—*everything*—for the preservation of this defenseless infant and the genetic information cupped in his cells.

That night. Mary and Louis in the sitting room, Mary typing a clean version of Louis's latest intelligence report. A shriek from down the hall. Ungodly sound. Mary's heart skips and then she is up, across the room, down the hall, has flung open the door to the nursery and rushed inside. In his cot, Jonathan's body crawls. Skin a red swarm. There is a hungry clicking, the cold shine of exoskeletons. For one full second she is frozen by the sight, brain unable to name what she has seen. Then it comes to her: *ants*. As soon as the word clicks into place she rips the mosquito net from the bed and grabs her baby into her arms. The ants, massive, crimson, hang from his flesh with pincers like shears. She brushes them frantically away and they latch onto her arms instead, biting, drawing blood, but she is such a wash of adrenaline she does not notice. Louis is there now, fighting the ants off too, and finally the baby is free of them, wailing like mad, skin ravaged by bites—but alive. Mary and Louis stand, chests heaving, waiting for their brains to calm their bodies down. In the nursery, the twisting insect column retreats back through the holes in the wall. A scattering of corpses left behind. Mary holds Jonathan tight to her breast. We are such animals, she thinks.

•

1941. The war rages on, and Louis is appointed curator of the Co-
ryndon Museum in Nairobi. Mary spends her days polishing her-
barium glass. Peter Bally, the botanist, has named all the plants after himself: *Adenia ballyi, Aloe ballyi, Ceropegia ballyana, Euphorbia
ballyana, Euphorbia ballyi, Euphorbia proballyana, Kalanchoe ballyi,
Sanseveieria ballyi, Echidnopsis ballyi,* and *Ballya zebrina.* He adds
specimens carefully pressed, bleached slightly like ghosts of themselves. Beams with a boyish pride.

Today, the only guests are a pair of British missionaries, nose up
close to the baobab exhibit: star-like leaves and a huge cross-section
of trunk, seven meters across and faintly ringed. Louis has plans to
lower the admission fee and open the museum to all. But for now,
it remains whites only.

Peter (*ballyi, ballyi, ballyana*) and his wife have invited Mary
to join them on a short trip to Ngorongoro. They wish to survey
some forests there, very near a number of Neolithic burial mounds
Mary has been wanting to see. The mounds were discovered some
years ago, when a pair of German farmers removed stones from
the cairns to use as building materials. Now that the war's broken
out, the farms lie abandoned. The burial mounds wait once again
unclaimed.

She has agreed to go. Jonathan is only six months old, but she
is itching to be back in the field—especially after emerging from
her last dig with nothing but a slag heap of obsidian. She has been
dreaming lately of that black chaos. All those jumbled tools. She
cannot bring herself to try and sort them out, and even if she could,
what use would it be? It is like a batter that cannot be unmixed. So
she has begun to pack.

Adansonia digitate. One of the missionaries, near the baobab.

The wife. *Named for French explorer and botanist Michel Adanson, it says here.* She gestures to the plaque, the text of which Mary helped to write. The other missionary, the husband, stretches his arms perpendicular to his body, comparing their span to the width of the trunk. *What a beast of a tree,* he says. *What a beast.*

1941. Her car parked above, Mary descends the crater wall on foot, a line of Wambulu porters behind her, carrying her gear and supplies. Some two thousand miles away, Brits and Italians gun each other down in the North African sun. A wrecked Panzer belches smoke. The soil lies drilled with holes. Twenty thousand conscripted Africans will die.

And Mary descends the crater wall, a line of Wambulu porters carrying her supplies.

1896/1941. The Suez Canal. Look at it, massive blue band cutting the land like a scar. And it is for this that 2,500 Indian laborers will never see their homes again, and it is for this 100,000 soldiers will die in the North African Campaign, and it is for this that the African soil will rupture and crack, with crossties and mortar shells, again and again and again. And it is through this waterway that a white woman will travel, from England to Africa to England to Africa, and it is because her country owns this strip of saltwater that she is able to park her car on the lip of the crater and descend its steep walls, her Wambulu porters trailing behind. And people will stand on the banks of this canal, khaki sand against jewel-blue sea, and they will point at the ships carrying cargo from one country to the next. They will point and share tidbits of history, the marvel of its construction, but they will not remember all these victims of violence and desire, hanging in the arid air like ghosts.

1941. She's set up camp on the crater floor. Her breasts are tender and heavy—still producing milk, abundant and unwanted. In her tent, she lifts a tin mug to her nipple and begins to express. It comes in beads at first, then quickens to a squirt. She develops a rhythm. There is a little soreness, but not much. The milk pings in the bottom of the cup, watery at first, growing creamier.

The first burial mound she chose to excavate proved to be of recent origin; less than two hundred years old, she guesses. But the second yielded more interesting finds: mortars, pestles, blades, beads. Three thousand years old, at least. A collection of ivory lip plates, such as are still worn in certain parts of Africa, and, she has heard, South America. Convergent evolution: the independent development of similar traits in unrelated groups. Given a similar environmental niche, organisms evolve in similar directions. Geographical determinism. And she knows this line of thinking veers dangerously close to certain outdated theories about race. For instance, that the tropical climate of Africa produces laziness and promiscuity. But she is more interested in what convergent evolution suggests about sameness—what is universal and inevitable. Distant bodies hurtling towards a single ideal form. And what she doesn't know but you should is that such thinking is as dangerous as any other. She wants to see herself in every other. Wants to swallow every outside thing.

Her first breast is empty; she switches to the second. She is thinking not of Jonathan back home, being cared for by Louis and the nanny, but of the word *cairn*. Cairns too appear in disparate cultures all over the world. Humans across the earth, piling stones atop their dead. And the other function of a cairn—to point the way. A tool of navigation. She thinks of Stonehenge. The flint of Hembury. All this language of rock, saying something, beating out a message from the past. And if she does not know what the message is, does that matter? Or is it enough to know that a message was sent? The content of life, so insignificant. It's the forms of life that matter, the shapes familiar and shared. This is why she's more interested in stone than bone. Less interested in morphology and anatomy than in the ways life slowly came to resemble hers. Less interested in the size of a woman's skull than in knowing if she carried her baby on her hip, the way Mary carries Jonathan.

The cup is full. She exits the tent, tosses its contents into the bushes. Brief bright spray, milk and moon. She imagines the crater in infrared, every mammal a hot glow against the blue.

1896. News reaches the camp: an outbreak of plague back home. Thousands dead and dying. Lymph nodes swollen, ruptured, gushing pus. Fingers, lips, noses, toes turned gangrenous and rotting. A stench going up from the flesh and British soldiers going door to door. They have their orders: *Should the inmates fail to open the door promptly, the search party will force their way in.* Those rich enough to leave the city do. *The soldiers will inspect all persons in the house in order to ascertain whether any of them are sick.* In the quarantine camps, corpses pile. *Should the Medical Officer, after examination, suspect that the case is one of bubonic plague, a segregation squad will be sent for.* Their belongings are burned in the streets.

For the railroad, the outbreak means a labor shortage. The next batch of men has been detained in Karachi. The chief engineer worries about Parliament, frustrated already by the slow rate of progress. The men worry about their parents and children and wives. They imagine their corpses, greenblack and crumbling. Working on the tracks, the men drop their crossties suddenly, stumble away, loosen their trousers just in time to spill liquid shit into the dirt. Their limbs bear wounds, infected and refusing to close. The foreman keeps his distance. It matters little, they think to themselves. It matters little what part of the world we are in.

1943. The baby lies dead in her cot. Three months old. Amoebic dysentery. Mary has stopped crying. She feels herself mourning, but she is not exactly sure what for. The baby, so young, had hardly begun to seem like a real person to her. What does it mean to mourn someone with no particularities? The body is very white. Small and stiff and cold. Lips open. Perhaps she is mourning what might have been. Foolish, she tells herself. The future is unreal. Only the past can be known and so only the past can be mourned. This is what she tells herself as she draws the sheet over her daughter's tiny corpse.

1945. The Red Sea. The Suez. The Mediterranean. The war is over and they are going home. There is a danger of leftover mines, so whenever her two boys are asleep she stays awake with them in the cabin, ready to rush them above deck should the explosion come. Her body clenches like a fist at every distant thud. Baby Richard has an ear infection and wakes crying, so she picks him up and steps into the corridor to rock him. In moments like these, bouncing her body in that familiar maternal rhythm, she thinks of her own mother, back in England. It's been eight years since Mary's seen her. Shortly after Louis began the Kikuyu study, Mary fell badly ill with pneumonia and her mother flew out to Nairobi to be with her. An Imperial Airways flight that took four full days. She was told, Mary knows, that her daughter was unlikely to survive. A fevered image:

her mother's mouth blowing on broth. She felt, even in the midst of illness, a pang she could not name. Love or regret or gratitude or resentment. Now her mother is ill. Dying they say. Richard has finally calmed in her arms and she looks at his placid face. Sometimes she imagines her sons as old men. Paunch and spots and pleats and wrinkles. Sometimes she feels very tenderly about this image, and sometimes she feels nothing at all.

London is broken. It is the coldest part of winter and the buildings are bombed and crumbling. The streets cratered, piled with bricks, scaled in glass. Later in the year, spikes of willow herb will invade the ruins, tangling pink in the rubble. The flowers will thicken and thrive.

Mary's mother dies two weeks after she arrives. Mary is out of the room at the time, and afterward does not want to go back in. Parentless for the first time, she feels unsteady, off kilter. As if some string holding her up has been cut and she is now free falling. At night, she dreams she discovers her mother's bones in the earth. She dusts the soil from their joints, glues their fragments back together, and is flooded with wild joy, with relief, until she realizes nothing is any different from before.

1896. But is it still 1896? The men are unsure. They are stuck perpetually in this year, in this swirling muggy year, this year of steel and sweat and sepsis. They should be able to measure time by the number of crossties laid, by the rate at which the country rolls by. This should have the rhythm of a journey. But it doesn't. Instead it feels like the inside of a globe. Like bumping up against the domed ceiling of a dream. It feels like hanging, or floating, or drowning. The years pass for the rest of the world but not for these men. They bring the sledgehammer down again, again, again. It is 1896.

•

1948. The west side of Rusinga Island, Lake Victoria. The sun just beginning its afternoon decline, painting the lake skin silver. Mary stands barefoot in the shallows, one hand on the back of her neck, in the other a trowel. Back at camp, Louis is excavating the bones of some extinct species of crocodile. But crocodiles do not interest her. She wants apes. She does, she admits it, she wants a direct ancestor. Not a side branch or an offshoot, not a skull fragment or scrap of stone. She wants something whole. She wants something human. More than she ever has before, she wants the picture of how things got to be the way they are. She wants a narrative, a diagram, some measure of certainty. This is a strange science, she thinks. A science of gaps. A science of chips and losses.

She dries her feet with her socks and then slips them bare into her boots. Walks back toward camp. The island has been a summer home for them for the past five years. In previous summers, they'd crossed the lake squeezed in among sacks of grain on an Arab dhow, or once on a fishing boat that promptly ran aground, requiring the passengers to be carried ashore by a group of naked islanders. But this year they have traveled to the island in their very own cruiser. A wealthy American businessman, reading about Louis's work on the island, surprised them by mailing a check for £1,000. *I have a particular interest in prehistory, and am besides a great lover of Africa,* read his letter. *Yours is a splendid example of British research on the African continent, which I hope this donation will help to further.* They named the cruiser the *Miocene Lady.*

Nearing camp now. The greenery of the shore receding, giving way to slopes of parched brown earth. Mary's eyes comb the land. She feels a quick twinge of malice, as if the ground is intentionally keeping its secrets from her. And this is when she sees it: bone fragments, their shape so nearly familiar, lying half buried on the slope. Closer. A tooth also. Distinctly hominoid. *Louis! Louis, come quick!* Soon they are brushing the sediment from the tooth. The soil falls off to reveal a jaw. They continue to dig and find more than half the skull, fragmented and warped. But *there.*

It takes several days to extract every scrap of bone. They entrust Heslon Mukiri with the task. *Seems most of the occipital is gone,* says Heslon, lying on his side in the soil. Mary stands over him, watching. *Think of it—eroded away, blown or washed who knows where. Could be in the air we breathe. The missing occipital.*

That night, Mary leans low over the collected chips of bone. For an edge jutting out like a peak, she seeks another slanted in like a canyon. Puzzle pieces, puzzle pieces. She slots the two together, applies a fine line of glue. Hold and holds and then lets go. The two fragments once again whole. Against such odds, what was broken now is not. *Just curiosity,* she said. *I just want to know.* But why? The truth is, it is a comfort to trace through eons of evolution, back to some sort of origin. To see that, through all the extinctions, all the adaptations, here we are—humankind. It makes it all seem fated. And to her, godless as she is, this is such sweet comfort. To feel that some force willed them into being. That this intricate branching of species was always headed to them. To her, here, piecing this shattered skull together. Of course, she knows such logic is faulty. Any random series of events will yield creatures to whom it seems anything but random. Humans are not exceptional. She knows this. And yet, it is a comfort.

A tiny crumb of bone falls from her fingers. She drops to the ground but cannot see it. Spreads her hands out across the tent floor, feeling, feeling. Nothing. She curses. The piece is minute, but crucial in joining two larger pieces. And even though she knows it must be there, must be, she begins to panic. What cruelty, for the universe to preserve this little chip for all these years, a piece so small it could easily have been ground to powder, turned to some anonymous sediment, but somehow, let's say miraculously, wasn't—what cruelty now for it to be lost because of a silly slip of the fingers.

It takes ten minutes of mounting anxiety for her to find it, and when she does, she is visited by an unaccountable urge: to swallow it. Ingest it and keep it safe inside her. Then the tent doors part and Louis enters, grinning. *How's it coming?* He runs his fingers over the half of the skull she has so far reassembled. Shakes his head slow in awe. *Come to bed. Finish tomorrow.* They retreat to their tent, undress each other with haste, not pausing for buttons or clasps but simply yanking fabric overhead. Panting hard, biting soft. *Let's have another baby,* he says, and she feels a quiet rush of rightness, as if yes, this is the only logical thing to do, this is the only thing. And they fall to the ground and fuck as if the species is theirs to preserve.

1983. *Perhaps it does not matter very much that there is this division between fact and fiction for the early years.... For later stages of the story accuracy will be far more important.* The period key claps the page and Mary gets up, goes to the kitchen, lifts the kettle from the stove. Pours a fresh cup. Returns to her desk to turn her story into chronology.

And as chronology is how I receive it.

1896. Eight hundred donkeys. Six hundred and thirty-nine oxen. Three hundred and fifty mules. Sixty-three camels. These beasts of burden carry supplies to the advance parties, who are busy clearing and flattening the earth to receive the approaching tracks. The chief engineer tried to employ local porters—Giriama, Wanyika,

Wakamba—to carry the supplies. But the men balked at leaving their homes, especially during planting and harvesting seasons. The foreman brandished fat sacks of sterling in their faces, but they would not be persuaded. He tries to explain in his report to the chief engineer that money such as theirs means little here. *Would they prefer rupees?* asks the engineer. In the end, he brings in the animals. They do not last long—fall prey to tsetse flies and dehydration. Fifteen hundred corpses, picked quick and clean of meat, outline the path the rail will take. The men observe the bones—strange humped camel spines, the diminishing bones of donkeys' tails—with absent emotion. They think of their own bones, scoured by hyena, rubbed white with a gritty wind. Think of their bodies joining the earth alongside these tracks. All the future passengers who will ride past, gaze out their cabin windows at the rushing smudge of green, unwitting visitors to a mass grave.

1948. Mary sits in a converted RAF bomber, the skull in a box on her knee. She is headed back to England, and the airline has comped her fare in exchange for the publicity of transporting what has been officially identified as *Proconsul africanus*. When she disembarks at Heathrow, it is to the black glitter of microphones and lenses. She sets Proconsul on a small table, kneeling so that she might point out its various features. Around her, the hot bulbs flash.

After a train from Paddington Station, she arrives at Oxford and unloads the skull before a swarm of giddy professors. The men peer hungrily down at the fossil, spectacles perched on their noses, and Mary finds herself standing in the corner.

Proconsul is placed on loan in the British Museum of Natural History. The Chief Secretary of the Kenyan Government writes to confirm the loan, emphasizing its temporary nature and insisting that the skull remains the property of Kenya and may be recalled at any time. Some twenty-five years later, when the National Museum in Nairobi does request the skull's return, the British Museum refuses. They insist it was a gift.

1896. A waterhole, scummy and green. Sukhjinder Saleem drains the water through his turban to purify it. It strains still murky into the pot. He drinks. Warm and foul. Forces himself to swallow. One gulp and another. Tries not to think of what the liquid may carry.

The water shortage has been going many days. The foreman sits in the shade of his tent awning, drinking coconut milk with whiskey. His wife nearby, twirling her parasol on a slow and slanted axis. The heat comes in gusts. A zebra skin forms a makeshift rug at the foreman's feet, and he stares at the maze of its markings, its dazzled zigzagged mass that leaves even lions dazed. The foreman's head begins to spin. Unable to focus. Unable to look away. He gets up, launches forward into the sun. There is tiredness and rage in him and, unlike the others, he is free to express it. He swoops down the line with notebook in hand, recording every minor infraction. He sees laziness everywhere. Men moving as if made of stone. *Roll call! Roll call, now!* The men assemble. Sukhjinder has just returned from the waterhole, damp turban already dry. He joins the gathering mass of men. The foreman's red face hovers above them and announces that, from now on, the men will be paid per mile rather than per month. Muttered groans pass around the crowd. *Now listen!* the foreman shouts. *Now listen to this. If you work efficiently, if you put your backs into it and no longer shirk your duties, you could be in a position to return home with a goodly saving!* Sukhjinder stares slack-faced at the foreman. Some men around him are making sounds of approval, enticed by the prospect. But he knows something has just been lost. Or not lost—taken. He knows this is just another way to treat his body like a bad machine. If it cannot speed up, it ought to be scrapped.

Sukhjinder Saleem is a man I invented. In the National Archives, big building of concrete and glass along the Thames. River light reflected in the windows, the windows reflected in the river. Sifting the record for names. The archivist pointed me to a web page on a computer. She was older than me and her hair was considerably lighter. The web page declared: *This guide will tell you how to find records of Indian indentured labourers at The National Archives. Please note that the terms used in historical records reflect attitudes and language at the time and may now be considered derogatory or offensive.* The web page declared: *It is not possible to search for a particular labourer's name in our catalogue. Some records may contain names, but these have not been entered into the online descriptions. Many of the records contain only the first names of the labourers, not their last names.*

The documents. Brittle and browned and two columns appearing like this:

—	—
—	—
—	—
—	—
—	—
—	—
—	—

The first column titled *First names*. The second column titled *Last names*. Hyphens stacked like empty shelves. And when an occasional name did appear it felt barely less than lost.

The archivist said she could help but she could not help. She ran her finger down the list of missing names. Her finger was longer than mine, skin softer, looser at the knuckles. Beneath her fingertip the names remained gone.

So I invented him. Sukhjinder, the one they call ghost. I invented Mary too but she is an invention of a different kind. And I have invented you and you have invented me and the archivist's fingertip is still sliding, sliding, sliding still.

1983. Mary has a habit and it is this: when her mind wanders from the tale, when the narrative becomes hazy at the edges, she fills a scrap of paper with her name. It is a blurry, reassuring thing for a hand to do. Mary Mary Mary
mary

               MARY mary   MaRy

Mary   mArY   mary

mary

m   a   r   y   MARY

Mary

Mary   Mary   Mary

      m

a

                  r

                       y

M   A   R   Y

                           M

•

1896. The Taru Desert. Bright white skillet barbed with thorny scrub. Temperatures refuse to fall even as the sun does; it remains over one hundred degrees well into the night. It is impossible to work, impossible to hammer a single tie until the water train has arrived each morning. When it does arrive, clanking and chuffing over yesterday's track, the men rush forward, clamber aboard before the engine has even pulled to a halt, begin bailing water with buckets and hands, filling their leather pouches, draining them, filling them again. Their limbs are coated with iodoform to treat their many open sores, and the ointment seeps into the water, gives it a sharp, antiseptic taste, something like the smell of a hospital. But still they drink, drain the train of every drop, then watch it retreat the way it came.

The crossties have been switched to timber, since the soil is believed to contain potassium salts that would corrode steel. Creosote seeps from the wood, sticky and gummy on the men's skin, near impossible to wash away. They feel like dolls of themselves, wax figures, statues. As if the blackish tar might cement them where they stand, mid hammer swing, turn them to so many monuments.

The Taru is caused by the rain shadow of Kilimanjaro. Moist air blows to the peak, where it condenses and falls—Kilimanjaro's cap of snow. The air, squeezed of its liquid, passes to the other side of the mountain all emptied and dry. This is the Taru. Cottony oxygen and soil like cement. The British foreman with his mustache and gun will think this phenomenon is a metaphor for the brutality and beauty of this country. He will think it a symbol of this savage and romantic land, a land of extremes, a land unlike others. But rain shadows happen all the world over; nearly every massive range robs its adjacent plains of life. This is a metaphor, not of African wild-ness, but of power, and of the things that perish in its pale.

At night, the men cremate the corpses of their fallen friends. Fires flare in the hot black, a moonless dark swallowing smoke.

Mary. There is Mary's life. There is Mary writing her life. There is me writing Mary's life. There is me writing Mary writing Mary's life.

Then there is Sukhjinder Saleem. Does he have a life? Does he have a writing of his life?

In the basement of the National Archives, I ran a hand through my hair. A single dark strand fell to the page below. Curled almost like a letter. Or like some fine scar.

The light was dim and the pages refused to speak. Walls and shelves rose up tall and looming. This place. This place. The wrong wrong wrong place.

Rose suddenly to my feet and ran for the exit. But the exit was gone.

1896. A telegraph clicks over the Taru to arrive at railhead: *Derail-ment at mile 54*. The foreman rushes back sixteen miles to find the great engine capsized. Wheels warped and useless in the air, pistons sticking out like broken bones from a body. Sometime previously, a rhino walked across the tracks, leaving its cratered footprints in the embankment. Heavy rains fell and the tracks filled like small lakes, destabilizing the embankment. Now the train lies there, cracked open, a body leaking bodies, gushing entrails of metal and coal. The foreman and his assistant help the passengers to their feet—African men, all of them, clothed in tan uniforms, boots, hats, equipped with rifles. Askaris: African soldiers recruited to serve the British Empire. Men employed by their colonizers to further the work of colonizing. This is what the train carries.

They are called the Uganda Rifles: 1,600 Sudanese reduced to a violent metonym. They believe, many of them, in their cause. *The Queen* hovers above them, an abstraction that has somehow invaded their bodies, and they swear their fealty to her and mean it. Or they don't. Or they have no choice. At any rate, the pay is too little and the marching too much. The men are allowed no leave, have not seen their families in many months. The British officers discipline harshly and without cause, unwilling to learn Arabic. *The Sudanese solider,* says one officer, *has great qualities and serious defects. He has soldier-like instincts, is brave, physically enduring and patient; on the other hand, he is, from his very patience, profoundly treacherous.* There is no money to feed the soldiers, the officers inform them, so the hungry Sudanese turn to plunder. They fight campaign after campaign after campaign, quelling dissidents across Uganda, erecting the Union Jack in their wake, until, eventually, the final indignity occurs: they are ordered to cross a stretch of terrain so waterless and vast it would keep them from their families for years. They file an official complaint, recite their grievances in newly acquired English, but they fall on deaf ears: the expedition must take place. The Nile, the Nile, and beyond the Suez, and India, and all the world—too much to sacrifice so that a few Sudanese might see their wives.

And so the mutiny erupts. Within days, three hundred askaris desert, marching west toward the Nile, where they enlist in whatever unit will take them. Unhappy choices. No choices. The mutineers are pursued. Rifles unleash their bullets. Months of battle, a long hot stalemate, and eventually the British eke out a victory. Sudanese bodies lie by the hundreds in a swampy field. Bodies gashed by bayonets, blood soaking bright. In his defense, the officer in charge says, *Sooner or later, a mutiny would have occurred, independent of any specific grievances. These Muslim soldiers are secretly contemptuous of the overlordship of a Christian power. The more ambitious amongst them secretly conceived the idea of driving out the British and creating a great Muhammadan kingdom in Uganda and its adjoining territories.* He cleans his gun. Resumes his march. The Nile waits, lush and bright and eternally bloody. And every other day, more troops arrive at railhead. Unpack themselves. Continue on their way.

All the trips to retrieve objects and bring them back and encase them in glass. All the digging digging digging. And then this shadowy basement, the papers stacked and spilling. There were no objects there.

˙ In college, I once heard a professor compare archives to the secretions of an organism. The papers slough off unthinkingly, shed like dead skin or old scales. They are not written intentionally to send a message into the future, but are rather the automatic byproducts of some other process—like sweat from your skin or smoke from a machine. An archive is like a fossil cast. A relic of rot. Of negative space. An outline tracing what's been lost.

People forget that the definition of *history* is not *the past*, but rather, *the written record of the past*. Rather, *the past as it exists on paper*.

I ran up and down the alphabetized aisles but still the exit did not appear.

1952. There is fighting across Kenya. An uprising against the colonists. Must the grievances be listed? Yes, they must. Very well: the violent opening of the country's interior, involving the murder of many indigenous Kenyans, the burning of villages, and the plunder of livestock; the expropriation of land, including seven million acres of fertile highlands set aside for exclusively European farming, while squeezing Kenyans into increasingly overpopulated regions; forced labor; low wages; high taxes; floggings; torture; rape; lack of legal and political representation; etc. etc.

The result: the Mau Mau rebels, devoted to achieving self-rule. Mary sleeps with a .22 under her pillow. There are bodyguards posted around the house. Louis, as an official of the British government, has a price on his head. He sits at the kitchen table, runs his hands through his hair. *Why did it come to this? To violence? The aggressive faction inevitably forces its will upon the rest.* Louis has been called on to resume his intelligence activities: broadcasting propaganda to the loyalists and gathering information about the rebels. *It's so difficult for me,* he tells Mary. *So difficult.*

Mary, at night, takes the dogs for a walk. Her pistol at her hip. She longs to escape back to Rusinga Island, where there is no violence, or to Olduvai Gorge, its surface barely scratched. It feels such a waste, this uprising, such a waste of time and life. Yes, the grievances of Mau Mau are mostly real; yes, the colonial government has made mistakes. But even so—

Someone stirs along the path. A Black man. Mary's pistol is in her hand and cocked in seconds. She is ready to shoot, when she realizes: it's her gardener. A heavy exhale. A little laugh. *What are you thinking?* she asks. *Out at this hour.* She pockets the gun. The man's heart is still thumping in his throat.

Jomo Kenyatta, a nationalist leader and old acquaintance of Louis's, has been arrested, and Louis is asked to act as translator at the trial. In his mouth, Kikuyu rolls into English and English back into Kikuyu. He is trusted by neither side. And yes, perhaps he makes a few minute changes, alters a phrase here and there to better facilitate communication. But his mediation is minimal. His presence, innocent.

Kenyatta is convicted, charged with masterminding the rebellion. He is sent to the prison at Lokitaung. Louis knows the region for its incredible sequences of sandstone and spectacular basalt columns. The sediment dates to the Cretaceous. *I am sorry you will not be able to enjoy it,* he tells his friend after the trial. *God knows why things end up the way they do.*

1896. There is a man missing. Evidence: a soiled dhoti at the river's edge. Fabric heaped and coiled in a sign, its meaning unclear but ominous. They search. They find the missing man. They do not find the missing man. They find a body stripped of flesh—head and feet intact, skin pale and marble smooth, but the rest reduced to reddish bone. Torso torn to bloody shreds. Limbs four grisly sticks. Around the corpse, paw prints. Leonine and huge. The men wonder—at what point did death occur? How much can be removed from a man before he himself is gone?

The camp simmers in fear. The foreman seizes his Winchester and strikes out into the bush, equipped with various ideas about himself, ideas about the steely glint of his rifle barrel, about what it means to lead and hunt and win. But he finds nothing. Returns to camp empty-handed. Assures his men there is nothing to fear.

Three nights later, a cry goes up in camp. Men shout, bang on empty kerosene tins, and the foreman with his Winchester comes running. Another man is gone. Monstrous grunt, brief frenzied shriek, then nothing. The second corpse, when found, has the skin lifted from the face. Teeth exposed in rabid grin.

The men fortify their tents with ropes of thorn and sharpened pickets, but the attacks continue, bodies dragged from tents and devoured with impunity. Fires are lit inside the barricades, oil tins clattered and banged, but the lions keep coming. The men grow reluctant to work, and the foreman must convince them that the faster the track is built, the faster they can leave this place. For his part, the foreman grows frenzied. He stalks the scrubland nightly. Straps himself into a tree to wait, but when the cry comes, it is too far off—he arrives to find nothing but a severed head and a few fingers. Sends the teeth and a single silver ring to the man's window in India. The next night he waits again in a different tree, a goat tied to the trunk as bait. Rain falls and soaks them through. The goat bleats sadly in the dark.

But this story is not going the way it ought. It is setting him up as a hero, some African Ahab, because yes, he does eventually kill them, a pair of maneless male lions—the Tsavo man-eaters. He shoots them full of holes and taxidermies their tattered skins. But not before forbidding the men to retrieve the scattered fragments of their comrades' bodies, forbidding any funeral rights in the hope that the lions might return for the scraps. Not before the chief engineer (who doubted the lions' reality at first, insisted it must have been the accursed coolies killing each other for food) issued a £1,000 reward for the beasts' slaughter, ushering in swarms of officers on leave, wealthy sportsmen from England, all hoping to catch the devils. Unable to do so, they kill dozens of other lions in the area, and the camp reeks with badly cured pelts. One hunter slits open a lioness and finds a slick litter of embryos inside. They tumble out, wet, rubbery, pink.

The foreman is angry; he wants the lions for himself. Builds a massive trap from discarded railway scraps and sits inside, offering his body as bait. He believes he was born for this. He has developed a habit of rubbing his thumb round and round his gun muzzle. Round and round. He imagines the beasts limp and bleeding. Imagines skinning them, digging his hands into the still-warm meat, slicing connective tissue until the lions are loosed from their shapes.

But we will not give him this moment. We will leave him, instead, in his tree. Rain-wet, tied up, bound to a bleating goat. We will let him exist there, in that damp absurdity. We will go instead to a sick man in his tent whose friends fled at the sound of a low snarl. Too ill to move, he lies there on his cot, waiting for the lions. They never come, but he dies of fright anyway. We will go to the Field Museum of Natural History in Chicago, Illinois, where the Tsavo man-eaters reside, stiff and stained and badly stuffed, sold to the museum for $5,000. Above the sad diorama, the wall text reports that thirty-five men were eaten by the lions. The victims' names exist nowhere. *The greater mystery, though, is why.* Curators spend years analyzing a chip in one lion's tooth, wondering if this defect prompted it to resort to hunting humans. *The greater mystery.* Decades of scholars baffled at such brutality. The museum curator says, *It's astonishing that, more than a hundred years after their death, we can be talking about not only how many people they ate, but differences in the behavior of two animals, all from skins and skulls in a museum collection. When you think of the hundreds of thousands of specimens upstairs and all the stories they have to tell…the value of museum collections is just astronomical.*

The foreman, rubbing and rubbing his gun muzzle. The widow opening an envelope—tipping her husband's teeth into her palm. A man staring at his friend's severed hand. Wanting only to set fire to it, loose its spirit to the sky, but instead being forced to watch it fester, rot, open up with holes. The tracks, advancing now at a panicked pace.

The labeled spines of boxes and binders. Dates, names. An order becoming incomprehensible. How long had I been there, how long since the archivist departed, and when would she return? I sat cross-legged between the shelves. Picked at the carpet. Tried to imagine the life of the archivist. Tried to remember the pattern of lines on her face. Thought of the faceless unnamed man I had come here to find but could not find. I felt him everywhere and nowhere. Felt his existence pressing its absence heavily against me. And as so often happens felt my own mind rise up like a great dark wall upon which nothing is inscribed. The lights in the archive went out, dependent on the motion of a body. I knew all I had to do was stand, walk forward, raise my arms above my head. I sat still and let my eyes play tricks in the dark.

1896. *Khabaradaar, bhaiyon, shaitaan aa raha hai.* The cry that floats from tent to tent. *Khabaradaar, bhaiyon, shaitaan aa raha hai. Beware, brothers, the devil is coming.* Supernatural explanations abound. That the carnivores can creep in nightly, never at the place where the traps are set, never where the foreman crouches with his gun, never where the men expect. Night after night. Man after man. The story strains credulity. *Do you believe in devils?* Sukhjinder cleans his fingernails with the tip of a blade. Digs out creosote, coal dust, dirt. *There is room enough for evil already. Devils are not required.* Perhaps, he thinks, we should not be surprised at this behavior, but rather surprised at it not being more common. In fact, he thinks, perhaps this is the least surprising thing—that every hungry, powerful creature will kill and eat and never get its fill. Filings of dark grit collect on the tip of his knife but his nails seem no cleaner.

1967. Kenya newly independent, Jomo Kenyatta named as president. Officials write to Britain, requesting colonial records that were removed from the country after Mau Mau was quelled. The reply: no such records exist. For years the records are requested and for years their existence is denied. Then, 2011. Elderly Kenyans stepping forward with a story about the Mau Mau detention camps. It is a story of beatings, castrations, boots stamped on throats and mud forced down mouths. A woman, accused of selling guns to the rebels, raped with a bottle of pepper and water. Tens of thousands killed.

A historian digs and finds the missing records. Fifteen hundred files, detailing systematic abuse. *If the detainees deny having taken an oath they are given summary punishment, which usually consists of a good beating up. This treatment usually breaks a large proportion. If this treatment does not bear fruit the detainee is taken to the far end of the camp, where buckets of stone are waiting.*

Forty thousand Kenyans bring claims for damages against the UK Foreign & Commonwealth Office. After a two hundred and twenty-three day hearing, the judge dismisses the case. *The severe effects of the passage of time on the defendant's ability to build a case make an equitable trial impossible,* writes the judge. *The severe effects of the passage of time,* he writes.

In another case, the plaintiffs win. In compensation for their torture and abuse, 5,228 Kenyans receive £3,800 apiece. *The British government sincerely regrets that these abuses took place,* says the foreign minister in his statement. Then he adds, *We do not believe that this settlement establishes a precedent in relation to any other former British colonial administration.*

1896. The camp hospital is attacked, patients dragged off, various body parts left behind: foot, arm, bit of ripped intestine. The men have had enough; they declare their intention to strike. When the train passes through on its way from railhead back to Mombasa, they rush it, five hundred strong, and prostrate themselves across the tracks. The driver hurries to apply the brakes, slowing just enough for the men to climb aboard. The foreman yells after them, but the driver has heard of this place and is anxious to get through it before dark. He lets loose the throttle, and the men shrink into the horizon, a smear of smoke, then gone. Only four dozen laborers have remained. Among them, Sukhjinder Saleem, who cannot believe anything better awaits them at Mombasa. At night, while the others strengthen the fortifications around their tents, he wanders camp alone. Half hoping for a set of talons to snag him, drag him off. But even so, he startles when he hears a sound, some snap in the bushes. He tightens, every muscle flexed and ready. His body wants badly to live. And for what? For this? Why does he cling so desperately to a life that cares so little for him? Biology's imperative is strong. No matter what, survival is the greatest good. And even when he does not believe this, his body does. Some snap in the bushes. He tightens. Holds his breath.

The dark archive. Listening to the hum of the building. Air conditioning. Computers. Could hear no footsteps, no creaking wood. Only a steady mechanical sigh. Lifted my arms, slowly, too slowly to wake the lights. Touched the boxes on either side of me. The next ones along the shelf. The next ones. Each indistinguishable surface.

In the darkened archive I forgot my name. This had begun happening at times, and when it did, I would count, steadily. To 102, 234, 317, 1,390. However many seconds it took to recall. This time I reached 2,000. 3,000. Lost count. Sat namelessly still.

I had been told that I would begin to struggle to find the names for things, but I did not know this would include the name for myself. It happened only occasionally, but was becoming more common. I was very afraid those days. I am still afraid. Though at times, lately, I wonder if there might not be something gained among all that will undoubtedly be lost. The moments between looking at an object and recalling its name have lengthened, stretched, and I begin to wonder if something might grow up inside this space, like wildflowers blooming in the wreckage of a war.

1896. And so yes, the lions are eventually killed and skinned and stuffed. First one, then the other. The foreman stands over the second corpse, riddled with shot, and commands eight of the men to carry it back to camp. They would rather rip the beast to pieces, but he forbids it. Must have his trophy. Must have his story—a story that makes its way rapidly back to England, a scrap of myth, hungrily seized. *When the jungle twinkled with hundreds of lamps, as the shout went on from camp to camp that the first lion was dead, as the hurrying crowds fell prostrate in the midnight forest, laying their hands on his feet, and the Africans danced savage and ceremonial dances of thanksgiving, he must have realized in no common way what it was to have been a hero and deliverer in the days when man was not yet undisputed lord of the creation, and might pass at any moment under the savage dominion of the beasts.*

The Tsavo man-eaters will appear in many films over the following century. Mustachioed and no-nonsense Brits gun the beasts down, stoic against a backdrop of Black and Brown men. Black and Brown men, thousands, recruited by the production companies, dressed in traditional costume, given no speaking lines, appearing in no credits. Black and Brown men, some of whom play fictionalized versions of their own ancestors, some of whom could trace their lineage back to the immigrants who built the railroad, or to the villagers who were raped and plundered, or to the askaris the train carried and released. The movies, a warped mirror of history. A fogged reflection, a skewed symmetry. The one they call ghost—*Sukhjinder Saleem*—looks at the dead lions, posed in front of the foreman's tent, heads propped up with sticks to suggest life, savagery, to evoke a story of danger and struggle and conquest. He touches one slack muzzle. The limp black lips. What do the lions mean to him? He cannot decide. They refuse to resolve into symbols.

And when in that dark did he come to me? And from where? The name all at once. Culled no doubt from the scraps of manifests. The few lonely lasting names. Or just something of my mind. In archival science, *provenance* refers to a record's custodial history— its original creator and all subsequent owners. Records of common provenance are archived together, and the integrity of records with gaps in the provenance is considered severely compromised.

At a time when names were beginning to elude my grasp, to have his name thrust suddenly upon me felt like a gift, similar to how writing feels these days. Somehow it's not as hard as speech. The pace of the page is easier, more forgiving. But it will not be like that for long.

1959. Zinj. Zinjanthropus. *Zinjanthropus boisei.* What's in a name. July at Olduvai and Mary has found another skull. Big flat cheek teeth and thick enamel. Pronounced sagittal crest, shortened foramen magnum, flaring zygomatic. So they call him *Nutcracker Man.* So they call him *Dear Boy.* So they call him *Zinj,* ancient Arabic word for East Africa, *anthropus,* meaning man, *boisei,* in honor of their wealthy American benefactor Charles Boise. Binomial nomenclature: the illusion of science. But it is all money and myth.

What's in a name. In calling the skull *Zinjanthropus*, the Leak-eys create a whole new genus. Louis admits, *Zinj does indeed re-semble the australopithecines in many ways, but exhibits enough mor-phological differences to deserve a new name. I am not typically in favor of creating too many generic names among the Hominidae. But in this case, it is warranted.* His colleagues scoff. In this business of naming, there are two tendencies: to split or to lump. The lumpers look for similarities between specimens to group them into as few species as possible. The splitters, on the other hand, are inclined to name new species based on only slight differences between specimens. *Louis,* writes one colleague, *is a supersplitter.*

They entrust the Chair of Anatomy at the University of Witwa-tersrand with preparing the technical report on the specimen. The Chair rolls up his sleeves, takes a deep breath, and plunges into this tangled nomenclature. By the end of the report, Zinj has been re-classified as *Australopithecus boisei.* Later, others classify it as *Paran-thropus robustus,* and then as *Paranthropus boisei.* What's in a name.

Splitters and lumpers. Louis feels a tug of disappointment when Mary shows him the skull: it is so clearly not early *Homo,* so clearly not a direct ancestor. So his consolation is to create a whole new tax-on. Clear division between this and all other fossils. *Natura non facit saltus.* Nothing that is is unconnected. And yet he wants something singular, something exceptional, something untouchable and alone.

And as for Mary? *Many of my colleagues expend a great deal of time and mental energy in reconstructing trees of hominid evolution. They juggle with Miocene apes, the various australopithecines, and with types of early Homo, sometimes making a simple evolutionary pattern and sometimes ones that are extremely complex. It is good fun, and an entertaining pastime if not taken too seriously, but in the present state of our knowledge I do not believe it is possible to fit the known hominid fossils into a reliable pattern. There are too many gaps.*

Too many gaps. A science of chips and losses. Gluing Zinj together, she thinks of what erosion has claimed. Thinks that what is
forever beyond her reach is precisely that for which she is always
reaching. Splitters and lumpers. What lies behind these opposing
urges? Splitters: a desire for uniqueness, exceptionality, fame, thrill.
The desire to make each new fossil a sacred object, to locate in
each one a *something* never before beheld. Lumpers: the desire to
simplify, streamline, to craft a straightforward story, a lineage that
can be held, an easy path to follow. There's only so much room for
sacredness, and one is more sacred than two. The splitters' tree has
no center, no clear origin, sprawls its mass of branches and roots.
But the lumpers' tree, driven to extreme, is no tree at all. It is a staff
or rod or arrow. It is a single point in space. It can be caught, contained, in any little and crumbling skull.

What's in a name? Zinj. Zinjanthropus. *Zinjanthropus boisei.*
Name it. Touch it. But can you do both?

It was autumn and rainy when I left. She was angry and I pretended
not to have the words to address her anger. I just packed up and
walked out and boarded the train and headed east once again, to
the city, to the new job, to this. She did not deserve it and I am
sorry for how it went, but I knew I didn't have much time before all
of this would be impossible. There were words to get down, there
were objects to name.

Yes. But also—I could not stand the look in her eyes when I fal-
tered. When I knew she did not understand the thing I was trying
to say. The sadness. The confusion. The distance. I could not bear it,
this sense of an intimacy going cold. I couldn't endure the thought
of forgetting her name.

•

1896. They have learned considerable English. They have learned to write their names in this other alphabet. Though the letters seem alien still.

Despite their progress, communication with the foreman, engineer, and officers remains difficult. The white men will not learn their language, and so the burden falls on the immigrants. It is difficult to learn without someone to teach them, without any adequate Punjabi-English dictionaries. They pick up words and phrases here and there, the ones most needed for survival: *hurry up, stop that, come here, what's your name.* But without much of a wedge to crack the language open, there is only so much they can learn. Sometimes, the foreman's wife gives little English lessons. She stands under her parasol and points at various objects, naming them as she goes. *Hammer. Pistol. Bullet. Book.* The men follow her finger, noting the names, trying to hold onto them. The foreman's wife enjoys this little game. Points at herself: *woman.* Feels powerful, doling out words like this. Then, after a while, she says she is tired and sends them away.

1960. He is a boy. Twelve. Maybe thirteen. Fragmented lower mandible with thirteen teeth, isolated maxillary molar, two parietal bones, and twenty-one finger, hand, and wrist bones.

Her own son finds him. Jonathan, bent over the land, revealing the boy's old bones. Next to him, Mary excavates a second specimen: this one an adult female. The brown ground like a mirror: woman and child above and below. They name the boy OH 7.

They more they expose, the more they realize this is quite a different species from Zinj. A larger skull, fully bipedal, possessed of considerable manual dexterity. A much more likely maker of the many tools they have found in the gorge. And yet, the remains are located more than a foot lower than Zinj, indicating a slightly older

age. Two species, in close proximity, separated by maybe a quarter
million years—no time at all in evolutionary terms. Two species of
early human, living as contemporaries? Every theory forbids it. But
Louis says, *Why should our species exist in isolation, when countless
species of other animals exist simultaneously? Time to rid ourselves of
this leftover religiosity.* And so they name him the type specimen of a
brand-new species—habilis, *Homo habilis,* "handy man."

In doing so, they change the very definition of the genus *Homo.*
Lower the brain size required for inclusion and instead locate the
essence of humanity in an upright gait and the use of tools. Behavior over morphology. If naming Zinjanthropus caused a stir,
naming habilis prompts a war. *I for one hope that "Homo habilis"
will disappear as rapidly as he came,* writes one Oxford professor,
and the inclusion of quotation marks around the species name is
a sharp barb. Another professor describes the species as *taxonomic
hell.* Years later, even Mary and Louis's son Richard will call habilis
*such a grab-bag mix of fossils; almost anything around two million
years that doesn't fit the robust australopithecine definition has been
tossed into it.* Eventually most anthropologists accept *Homo habilis,*
but cannot agree which fossils it includes. It is a category with shifting contents. A leaky container. Net with a wide loose mesh. Irony:
a species named for its capacity to hold, a name that holds so little.

Habilis. *Homo habilis.* Handy man. When our hands evolved,
so did the rest of us. Prehensile: able to hold or grasp. But also: able
to let go. What is it to reach, to point, to hold, to lose. Please hold
your child's hand. Please. Subject puts the other's hands in its own.
Hands are what is held, are what do the holding. A closed loop. Self-
contained. The soil spilling from her palms, like emptiness turning
solid. Look at me. Look at the object. Point. *A dictionary is nothing
more than a giant tautology. To get the thing off the ground, there must
be some way of indicating what words refer to in the real world.* We

are so many mirrors of desire. The bloody carcass, red-fresh antelope in the grass. Point. Point, and by pointing, survive. Delay the
shedding of blood. The violent crisis. Posit a mind not your own.
Substitute this for that. To point is to touch what you cannot. A
severed hand, left as bait. A single silver ring. Complex, hierarchical, sequential thought. Twenty-one finger, hand, and wrist bones.
Homo habilis. Please hold your child's hand. Please. Please.

So now I was there, in the basement of the National Archives,
searching for the names before I could no longer understand them,
and the names were all gone.

I'm sorry, I said out loud in the archival dark. *I'm sorry you were
born here.*

1968-1972. A string of lovers. Mary walks in on them sometimes,
at the house in Langata: Louis in the arms of some young bright
willowy woman. A student or budding researcher. She finds a letter, addressed to Dian Fossey: *I love you and love you so and there
are no words that can describe…* Increasingly, he travels, and she
stays at Olduvai. Likes it there, despite the dust and scrub and
monochrome brown. At night, she dreams of the boy and his
mother—OH 7 and OH 8—dreams of them walking this place.
Dreams there is water still, a cool and rushing blue. During the
day, she drinks gins back to back. Starts around noon and keeps
going as the sun lobs itself through the sky. Spends long hours
studying her fossils, which swim in front of her. She does not
know what she is looking for, turning them over and over in her
hands. Only she cannot stop holding them. What happened?
There was Proconsul and then Zinj and then Habilis. Champagne

and press conferences and Louis undressing her in her tent. And then one day Louis suffered heat stroke and his hair turned white overnight. She woke and did not recognize the man in the cot. Over the next few years, his body morphed, grew heavy and slack. Teeth dropped from his jaw. Two heart attacks in as many weeks. Mary watches him from an increasing distance. What happened? Louis, walking with a cane now, strikes out for the Mojave Desert. He digs wildly in the Calico Hills, extracting rocks and calling them artifacts. When Mary visits, she sees an old man collecting shapeless chunks of chert. He holds an international conference to present his finds, but Mary does not go. Returns to Tanzania, pours herself a gin. At the conference, Louis's colleagues say little. They listen, exchange sideways glances. They are afraid. Will they, too, lose their ability to reason? And without that, what do they have?

Louis uses terms like *lithic work station* and *ovate-biface tradition*. Holds up a spheroid stone and calls it *an end concave scraper with bulb scar*. But to the audience, the words are only floating on the air. And for a moment, the absurdity of the entire task swells up in front of them. How to distinguish between geology and technology? Between one species and another? How to function in a world where no one agrees on any of the names? Afterward, Mary picks Louis up from the airport. *It's all right,* he says, his body seeming small. *They accepted the evidence.*

1896. Hundreds of gleaming orbs. At first, the men take them for ostrich eggs. Then, getting closer, they realize: human skulls. *A massacre,* the foreman says. *Eight hundred Swahili. Slaughtered by the Maasai.* The men turn intransigent with fear. They have had enough of being prey, of watching their friends' corpses reduced to ash and char. They refuse to move until the foreman provides them with corrugated metal sheets to erect spear-proof fortifications against the savage Maasai. The story of the massacre will move among them, accreting detail, gaining speed, cementing itself in their heads so that even their descendants will know the fearful image of the Plain of Skulls. So that, forty years later, in the border town of Pussumuru, the proprietor of an Indian market will say to some passing travelers: *The Maasai require little provocation. They are a bloody people.*

What the men do not know: the Swahili caravan, delivering supplies to a British military station, stops for the night near a Maasai village. They are tired and bored, bodies riddled with dirt. And so they venture into the village, looking for some fun, and find it: two young women, sitting outside, talking and sewing. The men from the caravan seize them. Grab them, big hard hands coming down on arms and waists and mouths, ripping these women away from their home and back to the men's camp—where, for an evening, they use them as they will.

It is after this that the Maasai warriors descend and kill nearly all of the 871 Swahili men. It is after this that, in retaliation for the attack on their supply caravan, several British soldiers round up and slaughter whole herds of Maasai cattle. It is after this that the British government investigates the situation and concludes that *the behavior of the caravan as a whole was abominable, and that the Maasai received the greatest provocation.* After which, they congratulate themselves on their famous sense of fair play, their incomparable and dispassionate justice. But do nothing else. It is after this that the skulls of the dead Swahili are picked clean by scavengers, and it is after this that the railway foreman convinces his Indian men to fear an enemy other than himself.

•

1972. She stands with her sons at the Nairobi airport. Watches crate after crate of cargo unloaded before it finally appears: the coffin. He died in London the day before. A massive coronary. And now, he is in a box. And now, already, his body has begun its decay. Mary remembers herself wandering the *causses* of Southern France in the wake of her father's death. Remembers imagining a world underwater. She keeps looking at the coffin and thinking: *fossil box*. President Kenyatta sends a funeral wreath. *Fossil box fossil box. Foxxil bos.* The headline: *'Cradle of man' discoverer dies. LONDON—Louis Seymour Leakey, a British archaeologist who claimed that East Africa was the cradle of the human race*—cradle. From Old English *cradol, little bed, cot,* from Proto-Germanic *kradulaz, basket.* Basket. Fossil box. Caldera. A species named for its capacity to hold. A leaky container. Blank photographs. The boxes dissolved to termite dust, big obsidian slump. The spaces inside cells, from which fossils form. Square-foot cube of hollow glass and below it—and below it—

The weeks following the funeral, she dreams each night she is wandering the gorge. She is the only human on earth and when she opens her mouth the words are in a language she doesn't know. They echo off the striped walls. Winds quicken, waters twist, ropes of erosion lash the stone and turn it all to sand.

The Pliocene Era. Dry season giving way to wet. The soil, rich with carbonite and soft ash, turns sticky when damp. Animals—birds, rhinos, elephants, antelope, insects—walk across this soft soil and leave their tracks behind. Footprints: a presence signified by loss. What is carved out of the earth, what is *not there,* is the thing we want to hold. Trace a footprint with your finger and you are touching nothing.

On this overcast day, rainclouds thickening and stitching together, a mother and her son walk the length of the gorge. Loping limbs, smallish skulls, bright dark eyes. Their feet press into the ashy earth, tracks unfurling behind them like the string of a kite. The boy, falling slightly behind his mother, observes the impressions left by her feet. He adjusts his path to match hers, stepping where she has stepped, one footprint nested inside the other.

Days later, just long enough for the carbonite to firm up like cement, a nearby volcano, which has been spraying intermittent ash across the gorge for weeks, now erupts in earnest. A thick ashy shroud, descending to bury the land in layers of time. And in doing so, it fills in the many footprints, animal and human, covers them gently, preserves them. Years. Years and years and the carbonite is replaced by calcite. Soft mineral giving way to hard. Turning the footprints into fossilized casts. A fossil cast, unlike a fossilized bone, is only an imprint of what once was. A trace of absence.

1978. She has found the footprints. After 2.8 million years, she has found them. First, the animals: over 18,000 individual prints. And then, the hominids. Just four prints for now, two sets side by side, and she is anxious for the opinions of others. She invites several colleagues to come examine the site. Some agree the tracks are human; others posit some sort of extinct bear. Mary finds what distinctly appears to be the heel part of a hominid print, the front part lost to erosion, and she asks Ndibo Mbuika, one of her most experienced staff members, to excavate it. He reports back to camp that night, wiping the dirt from his neck and arms. *Definitely human,* he says. *Also, I found two more prints. One of them this big.* He holds up his hands about twelve inches apart. Tim White, a professor from Berkeley, scoffs. *You're exaggerating,* he says. *No exaggeration,* says Ndibo.

The next morning, Tim and Mary follow Ndibo out to the site. *Well will you look at that.* The new print is indeed strangely large.

Tim rubs at the back of his neck. *There must be more*, says Mary. *We'll have to excavate below the tuff.* Tim straightens up. *I think I'd better take over. This excavation will require great care and precision.* Mary glances sidelong at Ndibo, who is staring at Tim. She has never been able to convince her American friend of the competence of her Kenyan staff. Ndibo now speaks: *I take great pride in my level of care and precision, sir.* His voice is steady and low. *I'm sure you do, and you've done a fine job here. But time to let the professionals take over.* Mary feels awkward. Ndibo is looking at her. Tim is not. She likes and trusts Ndibo, but Tim is a colleague she cannot afford to upset. *I could use your help making casts, Ndibo*, she says. *A friend of mine is coming to show us a new latex and silicon method. It should produce excellent results.*

So Tim begins the excavation. Slowly peels back layers of soil and tuff to reveal two parallel tracks, extending for eighty feet. Mary watches in awe. Unlike Proconsul or Zinj or OH 7, the footprints aren't something that happens all at once—a skull you can hold in your hand and know, more or less right away, what you've got. The footprints emerge slow. Growing gradually in detail, length, and significance over last season and now this. It feels like a secret. Like a held breath. Like a trail of breadcrumbs that at any time might be turned to dust, pecked by sparrows, blown away in the wind.

Some of the prints are strange—large, like the one Ndibo found. As if they might be double prints. But Tim disagrees. He insists the prints are all single, and he excavates them as such.

He excavates them as such. Is excavation recovering what is there, or constructing it? What choices must be made, like a sculptor at his clay? The story Tim believes is the story the land is made to tell.

•

1978. *National Geographic* sends an artist down to Laetoli. They want to do an article on the hominid trails and want a striking image to print alongside it. The artist meets with Mary to ask her about the humans who left these prints. What did they look like? How many were there? Then he sets off to sketch. Mary envies him. When was the last time she made any illustrations? When was the last time she looked at a thing, not to classify it, but to imagine it?

So that night, when the rest of the camp is asleep, she heads alone to the site. In her flashlight's cone of light, tools and buckets of upturned earth cast long dark shadows. The footprints are little pools of dark. She props the flashlight against a rock and sits down to draw. The solitary beam paints the scene in chiaroscuro: she sketches with only graphite. Produces first one picture, then a second, then a third. They are very poor. The scene unrecognizable, merely a collage of greyblack shapes. The footprints look less like footprints and more like a message in Morse code. Dots and dashes. A language she cannot read. She draws a fourth, then a fifth. Then she puts her sketchbook down and climbs into the shallow ditch where the footprints have been uncovered. The final casts were taken this morning, the perfect silicone copies stored safely in a tent. From these, another set of casts will be made, and another, and another, until a dozen museums around the world will own these ancient shapes. Copies of copies. Casts of casts. A replicated loss. She thinks of her dead mother. Her dead father. Dead husband. Dead baby. Thinks of their corpses. Mostly skeletal. Maybe Louis with still a few meaty rags. She reaches out. Holds her flat palms in the air above the footprints, parallel to the ground. Then turns them so her palms are facing. Raises them, slowly, as if tracing the outline of the body that once stood here. That once stood *here*.

The *Nat Geo* artistic rendition is as you'd expect. The gorge, overabundant with flora and fauna. The two hominids, gazing wistfully to the horizon, animal body and human gaze combining to create something on the edge of familiar. It's good. Realistic. The caption underneath, assured of what it labels.

The season over, Mary returns to London. She has an operation scheduled: a hysterectomy. She goes under, and when she wakes up, something is gone from her. But she cannot feel it.

Then, in the dark, moving slowly, I began to pull boxes from the shelves. Hooked a finger over the cardboard lip and pulled. Then another and another. The papers cascaded around me, sliding down and over my head. I felt their flat surfaces on my skin. Like wings or tongues. Sheet by sheet I began again to discern the shape of myself.

1978. The study of the Laetoli casts has yielded the following conclusion: there are three sets of tracks. The larger prints are indeed double, created by a smaller individual stepping deliberately into the prints of a larger. A brilliant insight Mary cannot believe she didn't think of sooner. The behavior is so strikingly human—she remembers her sons, as toddlers, following her tracks in the snow. Remembers following her own mother's on a beach in the south of France. *Of course it's tempting to see them as a man, woman, and child,* says Mary in an interview. *But all we can say for sure is there are three individuals of different stature.*

Tempting to see them as a man, woman, and child. Tempting. Tempting because reproduction is the greatest good. Because any other configuration feels lopsided, wasteful, wrong. Man, woman, child. Man, woman, child.

·

On my feet and the lights flickered on. Running along the aisles ripping down box after box. Letting the contents lurch and slide along the floor. Letting disparate papers mix. Papers in the air. Swarm of white wings. Flapping like crazed moths. Electric crackle of the light. Thought of Mary Leakey's tea kettle screaming. Perpetual shriek. I lost my sight in all that page.

1983. Mary at her typewriter, ignoring what she cannot remember, forgetting what she has forgotten. The story of her life shaping itself like beads on a string: one thing and then another and another. Time is linear after all, and so is language. One sentence and then the next. A word followed by a word. Why pretend otherwise?

A language that unfolds in space—a language of gestures and signs. How might her story then be rendered?

The kettle screaming, going quiet. Her baby screaming in its cot. Another baby dead. Writing about the death of this baby. About the birth of the first. Writing about a future that never was and a past she has imagined. Beads on a string. Currents of steam churning. Fingers paused over keys. I create dreams for her in which she gets lost in obsidian hills. I pretend otherwise.

1902. The train that was built. The train that was built that claimed thousands of lives. The train that was built that claimed thousands of lives and separated innumerable families. The train that was built that claimed thousands of lives and separated innumerable families and disfigured the land with oil and smoke. The train that was built that claimed thousands of lives and separated innumerable families and disfigured the land with oil and smoke chugs across the countryside. The train that was built that claimed thousands of lives and separated innumerable families and disfigured the land with oil and smoke chugs across the countryside, carrying a pair of missionaries—Mr. and Mrs. Harry Leakey, the latter of whom is pregnant with her third child and first boy, who will be named Louis. The endlessly recursive, endlessly accretive sentence. The past that continues to spiral and pile and send out its shoots. The train, carrying the couple and their children to the mission at Kabete. A green wash beyond the window. Each crosstie a threshold between the future and the past.

When the train reaches its terminus at Lake Victoria, Harry mounts a horse and the rest of the family is slung into hammocks, each carried by a pair of Kikuyu men. The Kikuyu men carry the Leakey family the rest of the way to Kabete. The following August, Louis is born, and seventy-five years later, the Laetoli footprints are found.

Nothing that is is unconnected.

1896. The one they call ghost—Sukhjinder Saleem—stares out at the silvery shimmer of lake. The last of the track hammered and laid. And now what. The lake all hazy with late afternoon. The water brightly lapping. He can see the silhouettes of the foreman, the foreman's wife, several other white men standing in a clump at the rail's end. They have glasses of champagne. They are celebrating a climax, a conclusion, a journey completed. The arrow of time striking its mark. Blade into bullseye.

In his whole life, will he ever feel as they do now? That life has direction, shape, that there is some driving force compelling him? His religion teaches that there is a path to be trod. But he has just laid the path that will be trod, and it won't be by him. How can you believe in beginnings and endings when the shape you hoped your life would take comes undone? Just as the lions refused to become symbols for him, so his life refuses to become story. To believe in stories is something denied him. So that night, the last night but also not the last night, he sits silently around the fire with the other men. Nobody speaks. The fire burns at their center, and in the fire are all the ghosts of their dead comrades, their dead children back home, their dead mothers and wives. In the weeks to come, some men will go home. Some will stay. For now, most have not yet decided, and, sitting around the fire, they wonder about destiny. Many, like Sukhjinder Saleem, decide they are done with destiny. That the future is unreal and the past all too present. That there is simply survival, simply desire to persist. This is the only driving force, and whatever its shape, it will not be discerned by them.

Looking into the fire at their center, the men are in fact looking at each other. Through the reddish tongues of flame, their eyes meet. They do not speak. A silent circle. A shared gaze.

Sukhjinder Saleem is a thing of my mind. I am sorry for this, sorry I could not find him and so had to create him. Do you blame me? But I am not apologizing to you. I am apologizing to him. I am sorry, Sukhjinder. I am sorry you were born to be a ghost.

This note written on a stray page, while wreaking havoc in the basement of the UK National Archives: *The museum is a discotheque.* Did not know why other than maybe the frenzied records in the air felt delirious and right. Did not know other than I wanted to make something into what it wasn't.

Never a dancer myself though I would have liked to be. Closed my eyes now and imagined myself, another version of myself, a self I wasn't but could maybe be. She was a dancer. A body among bodies, light playing on face and hair, limbs losing themselves in other limbs. I am outside, at the bar, drinking a martini, watching. She is unafraid, laughs easily, says the things she means to say. I want her or I want to be her. Which?

The museum is a discotheque, I wrote on a scrap of page, and imagined a pulsing mass of bodies, suspended in time, outside of time, time pouring over them like sweat.

1979. She wants to make the footprints into an open-air museum, and even secures $25,000 to do so. But Laetoli is too remote—there is no easy road access—and she must eventually come to terms with the fact that a museum is impossible. *Well, think of the upside*, Richard says to her. *Now it's like your secret. It's like the moon—only a handful of people will ever actually see it.* And she asks herself: is this an upside? What is preferable: to see things few others have seen, or to know that the things you see have been seen by millennia of humans, going back and back and back? To feel isolated and exceptional, or connected and mundane?

She therefore does the only thing there is to do. She buries it. Covers the tracks back up, very carefully, first hardening each individual print, then adding alternating layers of river sand and plastic sheeting, an artificial stratigraphy, until finally she caps the site with heavy igneous boulders—piled up like a cairn on a burial mound. A navigational aide, should she ever need to find her way back. And also, a monument. There is a funereal feeling as she places the final rocks, as if she is burying not the footprints but the three individuals who made them so very long ago—or so very recently, depending on how you look at it. She is either chasms away from them or she *is* them—this is either crucially important or not important at all.

She mourns for her dead. She grieves the things hidden in the earth, the things that will never be found, or, if found, never correctly understood. The lost things. The many names, and even more, all that is unnamed. She grieves the words that do not exist, the ones that might have called this world what it is. Hers has been a life of reclamation, of preservation, of wrenching relics from time's grip, but the museum will not be built. The footprints remain where they always were, objectless objects sunk in the earth, and yes, she has gleaned knowledge from them, but what of that? *I just want to know,* she once said. Now she thinks, knowledge is unreal. Knowledge changes nothing.

What she would like is to touch. To hold. But she cannot touch. She cannot hold. So she retires from fieldwork and takes an apartment in a Nairobi suburb, where she sits at her typewriter in the wan light of a coming storm, Dalmatian sleeping at her feet, and begins to write. *I'm sure,* she types, *that an autobiography, like any other book, needs a structure to hold it together. Archaeologists often divide things into three stages, usually "lower," "middle," and "upper" if they are thinking stratigraphically. Afterwards, of course, they argue that the whole thing was continuous anyhow and that the divisions are arbitrary and for convenience only.*

Arbitrary divisions. Deceptive excavations. Photographs all chemical blank and boxes chewed out of being. The silicone casts in museums around the globe bearing the caption *Laetoli footprints,* even though the Laetoli footprints are so far out of reach. An empty glass case. A woman at her typewriter. Caldera caldera. It sounds like cradle.

Overhead, an egret releases a cry. Lucy looks up at the bright horizon. She has traveled a long way from the footprints, following the plaque as it wound and snaked through the grasses. She goes back now, back along that river of words, back through the twisted history she herself has written. She brushes her fingers along the words. Engraved in metal, they have texture and depth. They leave their atoms on her skin.

At the footprints, Dina is waiting. *So,* says Lucy. *They're only casts.* Dina says, *And if they are? I would have liked to see the real thing,* says Lucy. *How much of any of this is even real? Oh,* says Dina. *All of it is real.*

A wind picks up. The savannah grasses ripple like fur on a lion's spine. *What next?* asks Lucy. *Nothing next. This is it. Why are you always looking for somewhere else to go?*

They sit on opposite sides of the tracks, facing each other. OH 7 in between them. Lucy thinks: does it matter? Does it matter that we excavate the past, does it matter if we have the real thing, does it matter if we can speak of it? How can she lay claim on holes? Let alone doubles of holes? To Dina she says: *If you are me why can't I be me?* She has always needed a reflection in order to imagine herself. Reflection—a body made surface, a self without interior. Those moments she stared too long in the mirror and felt completely outside herself. Dina holding the bone. She felt fury and raging desire, desire for the bone, this sacred relic, but even more desire for Dina, to *be* Dina, desire to be that whole and full and real. And yes, yes, she knows: Dina is a thing of her mind. And yet—*If you are me why can't I be me?*

In the chapel. The insular feeling of a building surrounded by storm. Warm rumbling rain, mulling thunder, the roll of cumulonimbus. Two girls facing each other. One's face reflected in the glasses of the other. Lucy will remember forever how she reached out and took the glasses from Dani's face. The way her eyes appeared when free of reflection. Years later, remembering, Lucy will whisper, *We are not the same person.* It will feel important to say. Years later she will lie in bed and contemplate the shape of her girlfriend's ear. She will nibble this ear, gently, until her girlfriend softly stirs. They will kiss, then, and press their bodies parallel. They will breathe each other's names, and in doing so, they will believe, briefly and deeply, in something other than surface.

I have been a stranger to myself so much of my life, Lucy now says to Dina. *I have been empty and tetherless and without belief. And now?* asks Dina. Lucy gazes absently at the plaque, eyes sliding in and out of focus, words sharpening and blurring. She says, *I have learned to imagine many things. I have learned the names of many objects.* Dina nods. They hold each other's eyes a long while.

A soft sound in the grass. They look up. The *Homo habilis* woman, walking toward them. She goes to OH 7 and gathers him in her arms. She has no language she can speak, but she points with one finger to the footprints. Lucy and Dina follow her gaze. Then the mother retreats with her child, her feet filling the holes. Lucy watches until they are lost from sight. When she looks back, Dina is gone.

EXHIBIT: ANTELOPE METAPODIAL BONE (REVISITED)

And there will still be such violence. Millennia of death. So many killed and, so often, because men desire what others have. Language fails too many times. Or else it works in all the wrong ways.

But here, now, in the center of these humans: the red body. Jeweled with fat and braided with vein. An object whose realness they affirm without touching. Without owning. They lift their hands and point. The first time. The shared gaze. I know that you know. Ability to posit a mind not your own.

The many sacred objects. Bones and stones and even hollow space—footprints in soil. They are so rarely actually there. A fossil: trace of what once was. Impression, echo, ghost. Organic matter rotted and gone, replaced by mineral trickle. But while you can never point at nothing, you can point to that which isn't there. Yes. Yes, you can.

I have imagined you many times. Have you imagined me? We are both here inside these sentences. Yes, we are.

Making her way back through the rings, Lucy thinks: no—the oldest parts of us are not the truest. They are just the oldest. The lowest stripe of soil, so low, perhaps, it will soon turn molten and new. Hot thick liquid beneath the crust, churning currents, pockets of magma waiting to break, rupture surface, rain down again as ash. What new relics will be preserved. What new obsidian will cool.

She reaches the outer ring. Deserted now. Morning sun expanding through the room. There are glasses with melted ice and citrus rinds. The disco ball rotating slowly, throwing its shattered light. And in his case, OH 7, fragmented lower mandible with thirteen teeth, isolated maxillary molar, two parietal bones, and twenty-one finger, hand, and wrist bones.

Tonight, the throng will form again, rotating and swelling, circling and pulsing. Desire without object and movement without terminus. She stands there, in the museum that is a discotheque, windowfuls of sun sparkling off the display cases. On her tongue, there is a word—close, closer, beginning to form.

Acknowledgments

Many, many sources were referenced in the composition of this book, but I owe a special debt to *The Leakeys: A Biography* by Mary Bowman-Kruhm, *Discovering the Past* by Mary Leakey, and *The Lunatic Express* by Charles Miller. I am also indebted to anthropologists Eric Gans and René Girard, whose work inspired the book to begin with.

Many thanks to all those who responded to early versions of this book, especially Lindsey Drager, Jace Brittain, and Millie Tullis.

I am very grateful to the University of Utah English Department and the Dee Foundation for their financial support, and to the Taft-Nicholson Environmental Humanities Center for providing me precious space and time to work.

A huge thank you to Michelle Dotter for giving this book a home at Dzanc, and for her incredible attentiveness and care bringing it into the world.

Finally, I would like to thank my teachers, classmates, friends, and family for their years of camaraderie and support. This is, in a very real way, all because of you.

About the Author

Alyssa Quinn is the author of the chapbook *Dante's Cartography* (The Cupboard Pamphlet 2019). She holds an MFA from Western Washington University and is currently a doctoral candidate at the University of Utah. *Habilis* is her first novel. You can find her at alyssaquinn.net.